ALSO BY MARC DAVID VELDT

UNFORTUNATE EVENT

UNFORTUNATE BEHAVIOR

UNFORTUNATE CHOICES

IATROGENIC

Marc David Veldt

This is a work of fiction. Names, characters, business places, events, and incidents are either the products of the author's imagination or used in a fictitious manner. Any resemblance to actual persons, living or dead, or actual events, is purely coincidental.

Copyright 2019 Marc David Veldt
All rights reserved

For PJM

It is mine to avenge; I will repay
In due time their foot will slip
Their day of disaster is near
And their doom rushes upon them
-Deuteronomy 32:35 NIV

Chapter One

I think about suicide a lot. I will die by my own hand. That's the way I want it.

My death belongs to me.

When I commit the act, it will be definitive. Effective. Conclusive. Can't abide the thought of making a mistake and having some sanctimonious psychiatrist declare that I intended a desperate cry for help.

I don't need help. I don't want help. Not with my life, not with my death, not with my final task.

I will have justice before I die. Others will call it getting even. The more literary will label it retribution. The weak will bleat that it is senseless, criminal revenge. No matter. Something of great value, the greatest value, was stolen from me.

It is immaterial that the thievery took place because of carelessness and stupidity.

Are carelessness and stupidity more excusable than premeditated malice? I think not.

Chapter Two

My death belongs to me. Maureen's death belongs to others.

Strange, isn't it, that the people you trust the most are the people who end up doing you the most harm.

We met, Maureen and I, when she was 32 and I was 37. She was a nurse, and I was an assistant professor in the university's department of history. We were both veterans of failed marriages and unhappy relationships, and, when we met, neither of us were interested in permanence. She was beautiful and elegant and witty, and, to my great surprise, seemed to like me. Soon, I couldn't get enough of her, or she of me. Every moment together was magical, especially the sex. We truly made love. Both of us knew how unusual that was. Despite our vows to go slow, within three months we were inseparable.

We had six years together.

We didn't have children. Not because we didn't want them, but because she'd received radiation therapy for lymphoma when she was sixteen. The doctors pronounced her disease in remission when she turned twenty-one. She'd gone ahead with life gratefully, joyously. Her one self-imposed limitation was the decision to forego motherhood. Thought her physiology presented too great a risk for a baby, what with the history of a deadly disease and the unknown long-term effects of the extreme therapy its cure had required…She was, after all, a nurse.

Sometimes I consider what it would be like if, right now, I were raising her child. Our child. A person who reflected her. That thought makes me ache.

Nothing but caring for her child could turn me away from the path I've chosen. But there is no child.

We were happy in each other's company. Nothing else mattered.

Never got married—thought a ceremony was artificial. Something we didn't need because what we had was genuine, something that didn't require public affirmation.

Later on, when she was gone, the people representing her killer contemptuously referred to me as the boyfriend. Wanted to trivialize what Maureen and I had together.

That was a big mistake, both for them and for their client. He took her life, then his legal advocates condemned how she lived.

The killer and his official mouthpieces assert they believe in justice. They insist they seek nothing else.

They should tremble.

We will find what is authentic—their interpretation of justice, or my love for Maureen.

Chapter Three

Maureen and I lived, we worked, we traveled. Nothing tied us to home. Personal ambition certainly didn't. Neither of us had any desire to climb to the top of a professional ladder. We wanted to do our jobs well, of course, and fulfill our duties to people who depended on us. Didn't want to let anyone down—be it a patient or a student. But we never considered our jobs to be anything other than ways to earn money so we could live the way we wanted.

We wanted to experience as much of life as we could. And we'd do it together.

We visited great cities and small villages around the world. Viewed art museums, national parks, cathedrals, and historically significant sites. We hiked mountain paths in summer and skied mountainsides in winter. We drove cars, rode bicycles, flew in the fastest airliners, and enjoyed scenery through the windows of stately railroad cars.

We wouldn't have traded lives with anyone.

Then, after five years, Maureen began to experience fatigue. Extreme fatigue. We first made believe this was the inevitable result of our frenetic lifestyle. Said stuff to each other like, "We aren't as young as we used to be," and, "We just need to get a little more sleep." But, in truth, we were frightened. Maureen was only thirty-seven. How could this happen to a healthy thirty-seven-year-old woman?

We conspired to ignore what was right there before us.

Her physicians, the people who'd administered all that radiation, had never claimed they'd cured the lymphoma. They preferred the term "in remission."

Neither of us wanted to ask, "Does remission only last twenty years?"

Maureen's ankles swelled. Coughing fits awakened her at night.

She wanted to wait just a little longer. Told me she was sure it was just some acute process.

She'd never been a liar, and wasn't good at it.

I insisted she see a doctor. Never occurred to me that a doctor would kill her.

Chapter Four

We went to an internist's office together. The receptionist immediately assigned us essential tasks that had to be completed prior to receiving care. We displayed insurance cards, filled out forms stating we were both employed, and signed papers agreeing we were personally responsible for any fees disallowed by our health plans. Then we got to the most important document, the one declaring that, whatever happened, it wasn't the physician's fault. Or the fault of any of his employees, either. We signed that document too.

After we finished all the really important stuff, and after it had been checked by the receptionist for completeness, we received forms of secondary importance. The ones that asked Maureen to state why she'd come to the physician's office—her chief complaint. There was also a space for discussing her past medical history—little things like lymphoma and radiation therapy.

Forty-five minutes after we arrived, a nurse escorted Maureen through a doorway and into the examination room. I waited in a cheap, hard-backed chair and stared unseeing at a wall-mounted television set.

The same nurse re-entered the waiting room thirty-five minutes later. She nodded and indicated I should follow her. She led me to an examination room and knocked gently on the door. A man said, "Please, come in."

Maureen sat on the examination table, fully dressed. A physician, middle-aged and a little frayed around the edges, sat on a rolling stool facing her. As I entered, he offered his hand, but didn't stand. He nodded at a second chair, the one against the wall. I sat down, then turned toward Maureen. She looked almost, but not quite, relieved. Tears were in her eyes.

"I may have good news," the doctor intoned. "At least, I believe it's better news than Maureen and you may have expected." He looked at her, then back at me. "The examination today is preliminary, and I have to warn you that further work-up is indicated. Future studies will include X-Rays, evaluation of blood counts, and probable cardiac catheterization. But I see no evidence of enlarged lymph nodes or any other sign of recurrence of the lymphoma. What I did find is that Maureen has a heart murmur. When I put the murmur together with Maureen's recent symptoms, my tentative diagnosis is that she is suffering from a heart valve problem. This is something known to happen after patients receive radiation for treatment of lymphoma." He paused again, as if in deep thought, and looked back at Maureen. "I believe your heart problem may be curable with valve replacement surgery. I'd like to send you to specialists who can address your problem. My recommendation is that you see an oncologist and a cardiologist…as soon as possible."

I could choke out only a few words. "She's going to be all right?"

"I am very hopeful."

Now I had tears in my eyes.

We followed the internist's advice, just as we followed every other caregiver's instructions. Never questioned an opinion. Maureen thanked every caregiver for his or her help. She was the perfect, cooperative patient.

She remained the perfect patient until she passed away. Or, more accurately, until she was killed.

Chapter Five

Maureen and I never saw the frayed internist after the initial examination. Instead, we traveled from one subspecialist to another as we journeyed through the assembly line of modern medicine. The buildings, examination rooms, laboratories, radiology facilities, and procedure rooms were clean, neat, organized. Efficiency was the overwhelming goal, and pursuit of that goal was overt.

It should have made me comfortable, this obvious reliance on proven systems to produce predictable results. For reasons I couldn't then put into words, I felt uneasy. It was almost as if we were moving through the ultra-modern airport in Beijing—going where we were pointed, but not understanding the customs—or the language—of those around us.

I discovered, surprisingly, that caregivers aren't in overall charge. Not really. The system is run by faceless bureaucrats. Highly paid bureaucrats whose job satisfaction is entirely dependent on corporate profits. High corporate profits translate directly to high salaries and lucrative stock options.

The corporations pretend to care about patients' outcomes. To do otherwise would be a public relations nightmare. Can't let that happen.

Caregivers understand their place. They know who genuinely runs the business of modern medicine, and they play their assigned part. It'd be foolish to rock the boat—to do so would cost physicians their high salaries, their social standing, and their ego-centric view of the world. They've abandoned hope of influencing corporate behavior. Bureaucrats can replace an uncooperative doctor anytime they choose.

No caregiver in the system knows, or wants to know, anything except what relates directly to his or her specific job or specialty. You know, billable items. None of them express any curiosity about anything they aren't certified to review. They are never skeptical of another caregiver's opinion, plan, or judgment…It's amazing what an incredibly polite group of professionals they've become.

They've learned it's legally dangerous to stray from their assigned function on the assembly line. Lawyers have made that plain. Caregivers are more constrained in the world of modern medicine than are the patients.

It's a shame no one offers judgement about the patient's overall care. Or, more accurately, feels a moral compunction to do so. But, I guess, all businesses are like that.

The subspecialists and their technicians, some of them anyway, make attempts to leaven their professional advice with humanity—I'll give them that. But it's obvious such efforts are pro forma and strictly limited by the overwhelming necessity to ration valuable time efficiently.

None of them recognize that the patient's time is valuable, too. It can be priceless because, if a physician makes a mistake, that time is limited. Sometimes severely limited.

We entered the system and became part of it. Tests demonstrated Maureen suffered from aortic regurgitation. Further tests found no recurrence of the lymphoma. Surgery for aortic valve replacement was scheduled three weeks after her initial appointment with the frayed internist.

We were assured she'd do well and experience instant alleviation of her symptoms. It was the time-proven, effective treatment for her problem.

Routine.

Chapter Six

On the last day of her life, Maureen was scheduled third in Operating Room 5. Like every other patient, she'd wanted to have her operation first—believing the heart team was less likely to be fatigued early in the morning. But the first case-of-the-day openings were spoken for long in advance, so we accepted the opportunity to allay her symptoms sooner by accepting an immediately available afternoon slot.

At 1:15, the surgeon's physician assistant came to Maureen's pre-operative cubicle to check paperwork. He completed that task, then launched into a canned pep talk. He was cheerful, and we were encouraged. The PA said the first two cases of the day had gone well, the team was humming with efficiency, and he anticipated no problems with Maureen's aortic valve replacement. He shook our hands and strode away with the confidence of a busy, self-fulfilled individual.

Maureen and I held hands until two nurses came. We kissed. The nurses wheeled her down the corridor to Operating Room 5.

They took her to her death.

Two hours later, a nurse came to me in the waiting room. She said there'd been difficulties. I said, "No. No. No. You must be mistaken. Maureen is a young woman having a routine operation. Everyone says it's routine. You should check. You must have the wrong person."

The nurse spoke quietly, sympathetically, "I'm sorry. I wish I were mistaken. But I'm not. Please, sir, come with me." She escorted me to a private room. "The surgeon will come here soon."

I stood in the middle of the room. Alone. Waited for the surgeon. Knew what he'd say.

I faced away from the door and didn't look up when it opened. The surgeon slowly walked around me. Wanted to face me. I lifted my gaze from the floor. As I did, and this is strange, I remember seeing blood splatters on his shoe covers and small droplets of dried blood on his scrub suit pants. I saw a white coat, unbuttoned, and I saw his hands in the pockets. I lifted my head and looked into the man's eyes. I saw exhaustion, and despair, and sorrow. I also saw fear. Fear of consequences, and fear of me.

I whispered, "She's gone…Isn't she?"

"I'm sorry. We couldn't save her. We did everything we could."

"What happened? What happened to Maureen?"

"It's too early to know. To know for sure."

I looked into his eyes. He wanted to avert them, but, in an act of will, he didn't.

"You know what happened. Tell me."

"I can't talk about it. We have to investigate. I can't comment now."

"So you know, but you won't tell me."

His voice was hoarse. "The hospital has counselors. Or a chaplain, if you prefer. We will do everything we can to help you."

His right hand came out of his pocket. He reached up, as if to put his hand on my shoulder. I murmured, "Don't touch me."

"Everyone on the heart team shares your grief…"

"Leave me."

"I know how difficult this must be…"

"Leave."

I don't know how long I waited in that room. Time meant nothing to me.

I considered my responsibilities. There were two. First, I'd lay Maureen to rest. Then I'd find out what happened.

I was the one person in that gleaming, ultramodern hospital who wasn't trying to duck personal responsibility. Everyone who'd been in Operating Room 5—every last one of them—was anxious to hide the truth. They'd all be like her surgeon, who falsely claimed an investigation was necessary to determine the cause of death.

They wanted to bury the truth. I had to bury Maureen.

I accepted my responsibilities. I'd force everyone else to do the same.

Someone knocked tentatively on the door. I opened it. A woman stood before me.

I said, "Are you here to tell me what happened?"

She replied in a timid voice. "I'm not a medical person and have no expertise in medical matters. I'm a grief counselor. Please let me help you."

"You didn't know Maureen. You don't know me. You haven't any idea what we had together, and you won't tell me what happened. What good are you to me?"

"I know how hard this is for you. Let me help."

"Go find someone who can actually do something for me. I require guidance so I can take care of Maureen. Do it now."

"But, sir…"

"Go."

Chapter Seven

The hospital performed an autopsy on Maureen. Hospitals are obligated to conduct a post-mortem examination after any unexpected death. Routine.

I didn't want her dissected on a cold table in a morgue. No one asked my opinion, or cared about it. My opinion didn't count. I was only the boyfriend.

Now I'm glad they did the autopsy—their cold, soulless investigation. Didn't change what had happened, but it helped me identify her killer.

I owed her a dignified memorial service. Her parents, her two sisters, her friends and co-workers—everyone who cared about her—gathered in the chapel of a funeral home. Maureen would have expected us to behave well, and we did.

I wanted to remain at her gravesite until she was fully interred, but Maureen's mother and father disagreed. They wanted me to focus on what Maureen and I had together—the good times. Said she'd want it that way. I followed their advice and allowed them to lead me back to the chapel. Didn't want to disagree with them in public. Thought that would add to their burden.

The decision to walk away from the uncovered gravesite was a mistake. I'll always regret it. I should have been with her to the end. Never again will anyone prevent me from doing the right thing.

Maureen's parents believed we—that is, they and I—should grieve, accept her death, and strive to live the way Maureen had. We should be thankful she'd been part of our lives. The joy she brought us was the important thing. All else should be forgiven and forgotten.

But I reached my own conclusion about the past. The past, no matter how wonderful, does not negate future obligations. Maureen deserved the truth. I'd find it.

That night, as I stared into the dark, I thought about the conversations that took place in the waiting room after Maureen died. Replayed every word, again and again. Considered everything the nurse, and the surgeon, and the grief counselor had told me. And what they hadn't.

I'd determine precisely why Maureen had died. Knew the people involved would submerge her death under layer upon layer of misdirection, scientific jargon, and intimidation. Knew they'd attempt to mollify me with false sympathy. When that didn't work, they'd transition to staged and contemptuous resentment toward me—the unsophisticated, non-medical layman. Heap scorn upon me and suggest I was nothing but an opportunist who hurled non-substantiated charges in an elaborate attempt of legal extortion.

Then, when I got close to the truth, they'd try to buy me off.

Nothing they attempted would matter. I'd find the truth, and I'd act upon it.

Chapter Eight

It took a year to identify Maureen's killer.

I paid a lawyer to be aggressive, and he earned his fee. First, he established my legal standing to discover the cause of her death—even though I was nothing but the boyfriend who'd lived with her for six years.

Then he consulted a medical expert. This particular expert didn't wish to aid a plaintiff's lawyer. Or any lawyer at all. Why? Because he believes no attorney actually seeks the truth—much less finds it. The civil legal system is, in his estimation, nothing more than a no-holds-barred adversarial contest. Money, not justice, is its aim. Everything about it disgusts him.

My lawyer convinced this medical eminence that his client—me—wanted to understand the circumstances of Maureen's operating room death. So far, everyone involved had expressed sympathy for what they described as an unfortunate, unusual, and unexpected turn of events. Expressions of sympathy are not the same as explanations of cause. I knew the hospital staff felt sadness, probably even guilt, after they watched Maureen die—but I wasn't all that interested in their emotional state. What I wanted was a straight-forward description of what had happened. No one would give it to me. This made me suspicious. It also took the possibility of forgiveness off the table.

Pursuing a monetary settlement wasn't my priority. What I wanted—demanded—was honesty. I'd settle for nothing less. Truth, even an uncomfortable truth, was necessary. I genuinely hoped there'd been no wrong-doing. It would give me peace if that were so. In fact, I pledged to drop the investigation if the expert came to the conclusion that the lawsuit was without merit. I signed a statement stipulating just that.

In retrospect, asking this expert to look into Maureen's case was a stroke of genius. He is a physician's physician and is well-known in the medical community for his hostility toward hypocritical lawyers who file frivolous lawsuits. I believe he signed on because he wanted to demonstrate that professionals of good faith could police themselves. Maybe, just maybe, the medical and legal communities could learn to cooperate for the common good. In an ideal future, they'd jointly determine which malpractice suits had merit. Physicians and attorneys would investigate complaints purely on a scientific basis. They'd be empowered to dispense justice for both patients and caregivers.

It's a wonderful vision for the American civil justice system. Of course, it'll never happen.

This medical eminence unraveled the threads of the case. He spoke with the people involved. All of them. Then a most interesting thing happened. He became angry. Turns out, he doesn't like people lying to him. He thinks that indicates disrespect for his intelligence.

So he instructed my lawyer on who to depose, what questions to ask, and how to recognize inconsistent and self-serving medical testimony. Further, he offered invaluable insight into the psychology of narcissistic caregivers—and how to take them apart.

My lawyer asked the expert to testify in court—for a generous fee. This world-weary physician refused the offer, saying he'd fulfilled his duty by pointing my lawyer and me in the right direction. Instead of accepting money, he directed us to donate whatever we thought proper to whatever charity we thought worthy. We should do this in our own names.

I admire this man. For him, truth matters.

Chapter Nine

Three months later, my lawyer deposed the cardiac perfusionist. She controlled the cardiac bypass machine that day in Operating Room 5, and she'd been trapped. Just like Maureen.

This woman told the truth. Didn't hide behind claims of scientific inexactitude, nor did she try to disguise her role in the tragedy. Offered no excuses and spared no one else. Her personal pain was genuine. On the day of the deposition, she fulfilled a moral duty for Maureen, her patient. I'm sure she risked her career to do so.

I don't blame her for what happened.

Her testimony exposed the cause of the disaster. Exposed it for all to see.

I'm thankful Maureen had such a person with her in O.R. 5.

I won't identify her. We will call her CP.

Lawyer: "You are the person who was responsible for the heart-lung bypass machine on the day of the patient's death. That is correct, isn't it?"

CP: "It is."

Lawyer: "What is the function of the heart-lung bypass machine?"

CP: "When a patient undergoes certain cardiac surgery procedures, it is necessary to stop the heart. Obviously, when the heart is stopped, blood cannot flow to the rest of the patient's body. The machine collects blood before it can enter the heart. This also prevents blood from entering the lungs. The lungs, of course, are where blood normally on-loads oxygen and off-loads carbon dioxide. One of the machine's functions is to take the place of the lungs. The blood is directed to a device, the oxygenator, which replaces oxygen into the blood…Like an artificial lung…Then the newly-oxygenated blood is pumped through cannulas, which are plastic hoses of large diameter, and back into the patient.

"Pressure causes the blood to be pumped into the arterial tree of the patient and distributed to vital organs. This maintenance of blood pressure is the second function of the bypass machine. As you see, the goal is to preserve the patient's circulation and oxygenation. Oxygenated blood is supplied to the brain and other vital organs when the heart and lungs are nonfunctional during surgery."

Lawyer: "Thus the term heart-lung machine."

CP: "Correct."

Lawyer: "So, if my understanding is correct, the heart-lung machine fulfills two functions. First, it provides the patient with oxygen, which is necessary for life. Second, it pushes blood through the patient's body so the oxygen can reach vital organs and keep them alive. Do I have the picture?"

CP: "Correct."

Lawyer: "Therefore, it is essential that flow through the heart-lung machine remain uninterrupted at all times. Is that correct?"

CP: "Absolutely."

Lawyer: "Is it fair to say that, when a surgical team elects to proceed with an operation that requires stopping the heart, then that group of individuals accepts responsibility for maintaining the necessary oxygenation and circulation for the patient's vital organs?"

CP: "That is correct."

Lawyer: "The team accepts an enormous responsibility, doesn't it? I mean, there is no way for the patient to immediately regain circulation if anything goes wrong. The patient cannot save herself. Would you agree?"

CP: "Yes."

Lawyer: "How do you monitor the machine? That is, how do you know it is functioning properly?"

CP: "We constantly monitor the arterial blood gases—always check values reflecting the oxygen and carbon dioxide content of the blood. We also watch other blood content parameters during bypass."

Lawyer: "I understand you must ensure the blood contains the proper content of life-sustaining necessities like oxygen, as well as other variables, but how do you know that blood is reaching the vital organs and keeping them alive?"

CP: "We constantly monitor the volume of blood returning from the patient, as well as the volume of blood and fluid we pump back into the patient. Pressures in all lines are monitored and maintained in a safe range."

Lawyer: "You have determined beforehand the amount of blood the patient must receive? That is, how much blood she should receive each minute?"

CP: "Yes. It's a mathematical formula."

Lawyer: "A tested and trusted formula?"

CP: "Yes. Tested and perfected over many years."

Lawyer: "What happens if you are dissatisfied with the amount of blood the patient is receiving?"

CP: "We increase our pump flow by increasing the revolutions of the machine's roller. We can force more blood forward."

Lawyer: "What would cause failure of the machine to maintain adequate flow for a particular patient?"

CP: "There could be a kink or bend in one of the cannulas leading back to the patient. Or there could be an obstruction inside the cannula."

Lawyer: "What would you do if a line were, as you say, kinked?"

CP: "We'd straighten it out immediately."

Lawyer: "What about the other scenario? Obstruction inside the cannula itself?"

CP: "That is more difficult. Once you are on bypass, you're committed. Can't just immediately change cannulas. It'd take too long. Can't let organs go long without oxygenated blood."

Lawyer: "What would cause such an internal obstruction? I'm asking what you, an experienced cardiac-bypass perfusionist, fear most. I ask this because obstruction inside the cannula system seems to be an almost insoluble problem."

CP: "We fear the formation of blood clots. Blood clots compromise the machine's ability to keep blood flowing smoothly into the patient. If that were not bad enough, small blood clots will pass through the machine. These clots get pumped into the patient's circulation. There they obstruct the patient's arterial tree so blood cannot reach its intended destination—the vital organs. Those organs are then starved for oxygen."

Lawyer: "What do you do to prevent such a calamitous event?"

CP: "We administer heparin to the patient."

Lawyer: "Heparin prevents blood from clotting?"

CP: "Yes."

Lawyer: "Is there a formula for the heparin you, or other members of the operating room team, administer?"

CP: "Yes. In our operating room we administer 500 units of heparin per kilogram weight of the patient."

Lawyer: "Does every patient react the same way to heparin?"

CP: "No."

Lawyer: "How do you know the patient is reacting appropriately?"

CP: "We constantly measure a test called the Activating Clotting Time, or ACT. It's a reflection of the time it takes blood to clot. The ACT must be kept above 480 seconds on bypass."

Lawyer: "What happens if the ACT falls below that level?"

CP: "We administer more heparin."

Lawyer: "Who gives the heparin?"

CP: "In our operating room, we report the ACT to the anesthesiologist. He gives us a syringe of the drug and we put it into the flow of the heart-lung machine."

Lawyer: "Now I'm going to move from the theoretical to the actual. On the day in question, a patient died on bypass in Operating Room 5. I want to learn what happened."

CP: "Understood."

Lawyer: "It seems obvious that unexpected clotting of blood is a possible cause for her death. Would you agree?"

CP: "Yes."

Lawyer: "I want to make sure I fully understand how blood clots could cause such an unfortunate event. Now, blood clots obstruct fluid flow because they stick together and make the functional diameter of the cannula smaller. Is that correct?"

CP: "Yes."

Lawyer: "Do blood clots have any other effect on the heart-lung bypass machine?"

CP: "The clotting also causes fluid flow to become turbulent."

Lawyer: "So not only is there less flow, it's a more turbulent flow. That doesn't sound good."

CP: "It's not good."

Lawyer: "During the operation during which Maureen entrusted her life to your hospital's heart team, could blood clots have caused her tragic outcome?"

CP: "Yes."

Lawyer: "We've discussed the deleterious effects clots have on blood flow. Are other complications possible should blood clotting occur while a patient is on heart-lung bypass?"

CP: "Yes."

Lawyer: "What are they?"

CP: "Clots make the oxygenator less efficient."

Lawyer: "That's of vital concern, isn't it?"

CP: "Yes."

Lawyer: "So, a mistake in the level of heparin can result in the formation of blood clots. Such an event adversely affects the heart-lung bypass machine in two ways. First, the amount of blood returned to the patient is decreased, and, second, the blood has a lower than normal content of oxygen. Is that correct?"

CP: "Yes."

Lawyer: "Did that happen to Maureen?"

CP: "I—I'm—I'm not sure."

A sob is audible on the tape.

There's a pause. It's the first time my aggressive lawyer didn't launch an immediate question after a response from CP.

Two minutes later, the questioning resumes.

Lawyer: "How long do vital organs, like the brain, live if they don't receive adequate flow of blood? Especially if the blood is not properly oxygenated?"

CP: "Not long at all. Just a very few minutes. Especially the brain."

Lawyer: "Is there anything that can be done if this occurs? For instance, can you administer more heparin, or immediately replace the cannulas leading to the patient, or even replace the entire heart-lung bypass machine?"

CP: "I don't believe so. When you are talking about brain death due to inadequate supply of blood flow and oxygen…It just happens too fast. People will try everything in desperation, but, tragically, it's all over."

Lawyer: "Do you know this from personal experience?"

CP: "Yes."

At this point the formal deposition again pauses. In an almost clinical voice, cold and unemotional, someone states that the lawyers have agreed to a half hour break.

CP had requested a break. She needed to gather herself.

Chapter Ten

The deposition resumes.

Lawyer: "This is difficult for you. Obviously, it stirs deep emotions…Are you able to continue?"

CP: "I am."

Lawyer: "I intend to discuss what went on in Operating Room 5 the day Maureen died."

CP: "Go ahead."

Lawyer: "Did you meet Maureen before her surgery?"

CP: "I didn't talk to her. I was completing the set-up for the bypass machine when she entered the operating room."

Lawyer: "So you had no personal interaction with her?"

CP: "I didn't talk to her. I looked up when she entered the room. She was on a transport cart, and she looked sleepy. She'd obviously received a sedative. I was surprised when I saw her face. She looked so much younger than our usual patients in the heart room. I could hear the short conversation she had with nurses as she moved herself onto the operating table. She was awake enough to do that. She was pleasant and cooperative. Made some joke about being a nurse herself. Said she didn't want to cause any trouble…" There is a catch in CP's voice and a pause in the deposition's recording. CP finally went on, "I'm sorry. It's hard to talk about this."

Lawyer: "I'm sorry I have to make you relive that awful day."

CP: "Don't be sorry for me." Another pause. "I'm still alive. Be sorry for her."

Lawyer: "Did the case proceed in the usual manner?"

CP: "Yes. No problem at all. The anesthesiologist easily placed the lines necessary for monitoring her. He induced anesthesia smoothly. The nurses prepped her chest, surgery began, the surgeon rapidly gained access to the heart. Everything was routine. Just like it's been hundreds of times in my experience. The anesthesiologist gave the heparin. We went on bypass. Smooth as silk."

Lawyer: "When did things become different than usual?"

CP: "We check ACT's every thirty minutes. The second time I checked it, it had fallen to 490. I didn't expect it to drop to that level so soon, so I reported it to the anesthesiologist and the surgeon. They acknowledged the ACT results. The anesthesiologist said, 'I think we should add ten thousand units of heparin.' The surgeon said, "I agree.'"

Lawyer: "Is this, in any way, unusual?"

CP: "Well, the ACT was lower than I expected it to be, but, you know, that's why we check every half hour. Patients react differently to drugs."

Lawyer: "Was the order to give an additional ten thousand units of heparin what you expected?"

CP: "Yes."

Lawyer: "Who administered the drug?"

CP: "I did."

Lawyer: "Who gave you the drug?"

CP: "The anesthesiologist gave it to me."

Lawyer: "Anything unusual about that?"

CP: "The only unusual thing was that he handed me a syringe that wasn't labeled."

Lawyer: "Is that unusual?"

CP: "Yes. I refused to give the drug, handed the syringe back to him, and said I would not give the contents of an unlabeled syringe to a patient."

Lawyer: "What did the anesthesiologist do?"

CP: "He said, 'For Pete's sake.' He took the syringe back from me, slapped a label on it, and wrote Heparin 10,000 units on the label. Then he shoved it back at me."

Lawyer: "So you believed this syringe contained heparin?"

CP: "Yes. Of course I did."

Lawyer: "I'd like to make one thing clear. Administration of the drug is the anesthesiologist's responsibility. You just carried out his order. Correct?"

CP: "Yes."

Lawyer: "How is the drug administered?"

CP: "I pushed it into a line running to the bypass machine. The drug went into the reservoir, which is the container from which the machine pulls blood. The blood leaves the reservoir, goes through the pump, is routed through the oxygenator, and, finally, flows into the patient."

Lawyer: "What happened?"

CP: "Nothing happened for maybe five minutes. Then I noticed the tubing in the reservoir moving around, kind of jumping."

Lawyer: "What caused that?"

CP: "Blood clots. There were blood clots on the venous side of the pump."

Lawyer: "You knew immediately this was bad?"

CP: "It's as bad as anything can get."

Lawyer: "What did you do?"

CP: "I immediately informed the surgeon that there were clots in the machine."

Lawyer: "What else happened?"

CP: "The oxygen content of the blood fell precipitously and the blood flow to the patient decreased."

Lawyer: "What caused those complications?"

CP: "Blood clots compromised the efficiency of the oxygenator. It couldn't oxygenate the blood fully anymore. As far as the volume of fluid flowing to the patient, blood clots made the effective cross-sectional area of the cannula leading to the patient smaller. So less blood could pass through. Soon, as immediate end-organ hypoxia developed, Maureen's blood pressure collapsed."

Lawyer: "You use the term hypoxia. Make me, a layman, understand what that means."

CP: "It means the organs are injured or dying from lack of oxygen."

Lawyer: "Did all the blood in the machine clot?"

CP: "No. But enough did to destroy the effectiveness of the pump."

Lawyer: "What did the team do to remedy the situation?"

CP: "We gave more heparin. We called for a new bypass machine. We prepared to put new cannulas into the patient."

Lawyer: "Did anything work?"

CP: "No...The patient had low flow. She had poorly oxygenated blood. We knew she was gone. Dead from brain hypoxia." There is another pause on the tape. A long silence. "We were helpless...And she died."

Lawyer: "What do you believe happened?"

CP: "There was an internal investigation. They came to a conclusion. I think you should ask the physicians who took part in that inquiry to testify."

Lawyer: "Do you know what the physicians' verdict was?"

CP: "Yes."

Lawyer: "You have your attorney sitting right next to you. Ask him if you can answer my question."

A voice says, "You may tell him."

CP: "The drug I administered while the patient was on bypass, the drug I was told was heparin, was, in fact, not heparin."

Lawyer: "What drug was it?"

CP: "Protamine."

Lawyer: "What does protamine do?"

CP: "It reverses the effect of heparin."

Lawyer: "If the heparin is reversed, do blood clots form?"

CP: "Yes."

Lawyer: "When is protamine normally used?"

CP: "At the end of the operation."

Lawyer: "Why is it used?"

CP: "Heparin must be reversed because, if it isn't reversed, the patient will suffer from severe bleeding post-operatively. If there is a high level of heparin in her circulation, the patient wouldn't be able to clot. She'd bleed severely after the operation from her surgical incisions."

Lawyer: "So the patient requires protamine after she comes off bypass. But not before. Is this correct?"

CP: "Yes."

Lawyer: "I want to make sure I understand this. Heparin is necessary to prevent life-threatening clotting of blood while the patient is on the heart-lung bypass machine. Correct?"

CP: "Yes."

Lawyer: "And it is also true that protamine promotes formation of clots, which is important after the patient is taken off bypass. But because of that very quality, the promotion of blood clotting, protamine should never be given to a patient who is still on bypass. Is that correct?"

CP: "Yes."

Lawyer: "How could this happen? Why would the anesthesiologist hand you a syringe of protamine instead of a syringe of heparin?"

CP: "That's a question you'll have to ask him yourself."

Lawyer: "Rest assured, I will."

Chapter Eleven

Dr. Edward Porter, board certified anesthesiologist with eleven years of private practice experience, underwent his deposition forty-five days after CP. Deposition is a misleading legal term. It doesn't convey the true goal of the exercise. More accurately, Dr. Porter was obligated to explain Maureen's death.

We granted him an opportunity to describe—and request forgiveness for—the error that killed Maureen in Operating Room 5.

I expected him to portray the pressures he faced every day as he fought death in the open heart room. Present himself as a battle-weary physician who always did his best. Someone who might be worthy of forgiveness because he'd made only this one mistake after years of exemplary service for his fellow man.

Did I expect him to express deep remorse? Of course I did. Could any decent person do less?

I assumed he'd acknowledge his mistake and make an emotional plea for absolution. The acceptance of enormous personal responsibility is compelling. It elicits understanding and sympathy. The listener often thinks, "There, but for the grace of God, go I."

Dr. Porter would have been wise to confess, even if he were insincere. I mean, we had him. He had no way out. But, somehow—and this is remarkable—he believed he could disguise his culpability for Maureen's death. He thought he'd accomplish this with lies. His attitude can only be described as astonishing.

Porter writes M.D. after his name, but he possesses no understanding of human nature.

People are pretty consistent. Most survivors want to forgive…Even me.

At least, I used to.

Victims want the truth because they are entitled to it. Truth is the prerequisite for forgiveness.

But a liar believes he can get away with deception. He believes this because he thinks the sufferer is a fool.

I am not a fool.

Dr. Porter signed his own death warrant the day of his deposition.

The bulk of Porter's legal examination was the scripted dance common—and apparently necessary—when lawyers attempt to score points. The important part of the deposition took only minutes to complete. You can draw your own conclusions about the doctor's character…I certainly did.

Lawyer: "What circumstances led to this patient's death?"

Porter: "The heart-lung bypass machine was unable to sustain her life."

Lawyer: "Why did this happen?"

Porter: "It is possible that the blood running through the machine partially clotted."

Lawyer: "Why did that happen?"

Porter: "I don't know."

Lawyer: "You don't know?"

Porter: "No."

Lawyer: "Is it not true, Doctor, that a committee of physicians looked into this event?"

Porter: "Yes."

Lawyer: "Did they reach a conclusion?"

Porter: "Yes."

Lawyer: "What was that conclusion?"

Porter: "I am not at liberty to discuss that."

Lawyer: "Why not?"

Porter: "The conclusions of the quality assurance committee are protected by law."

Lawyer: "Why is that?"

Porter: "Because no one would talk freely to such a committee if his or her testimony, or the committee's conclusions, were open to discovery by lawyers."

Lawyer: "Physicians fear such knowledge would put their colleagues, or themselves, in legal jeopardy. Is that correct?"

Porter: "You would have to consult attorneys representing the hospital for a legal interpretation of quality assurance rules and regulations."

Lawyer: "I have done so. But today I'd like to learn your impression of why this patient's—her name was Maureen, by the way—why her blood suddenly began to clot while she was on bypass. This is a highly unusual event, is it not?"

Porter: "I do not wish to speculate."

Lawyer: "Isn't it true that, if the dose of heparin were inadequate, the routine testing of Activated Clotting Time would pick up an adverse trend that could be treated before a disaster could occur?"

Porter: "That is what we, as physicians, hope."

Lawyer: "But, in this case, the patient developed a sudden—a very sudden—increased coagulation of her blood. That is true, is it not?"

Porter: "That may be true. There are no certainties in medicine."

Lawyer: "We have testimony that the increased coagulation of the blood was caused by the administration of the drug Protamine. Do you believe that's what happened?"

Porter: "I do not wish to speculate."

Lawyer: "The disaster occurred within five minutes after the administration of a syringe of medication. The drug was injected by the cardiac perfusionist. The perfusionist received that syringe from you. She says you handed her an unlabeled syringe and, when she refused to give the medication contained in that unlabeled syringe, you took the syringe back from her and labeled it Heparin, 10,000 units. Is that true?"

Porter: "I gave her a syringe containing Heparin and labeled Heparin."

Lawyer: "But, if the disaster occurred within five minutes of the injection of that syringe's contents, it is probable that Heparin was not what the syringe contained. In fact, experts tell me that the time frame and results point to Protamine as the drug most likely given. Do you agree with that?"

Porter: "I do not wish to speculate."

Lawyer: "You are the person responsible for the administration of medications during bypass. Is that true?"

Porter: "I am."

Lawyer: "What circumstances would cause the injection of the wrong drug?"

Porter: "I don't know. I gave the correct drug to the perfusionist. If there was a mistake after I handed her a syringe, the most likely scenario is that she mixed up the syringe after I handed it to her."

Lawyer: "So you accept no responsibility?"

Porter: "I am responsible only for my own actions."

Lawyer: "Do you expect me, and the court, to believe that a competent perfusionist took a syringe from your hands and somehow substituted a different syringe before she immediately administered the drug? That sounds like a preposterous supposition."

Porter: "Read the literature. Nurses, perfusionists, medical technicians, and the like make medication mistakes often. There are medical journal articles that discuss this."

Lawyer: "Your defense is imaginative. I'll give you that…Are you still credentialed to work in the heart room?"

Porter: "My credentials for open heart anesthesia have been temporarily suspended. This is a routine and temporary administrative action that takes place after any unexplained death in the cardiac surgery room."

Lawyer: "It's been well over a year since the patient died. It seems a very long time for a temporary suspension. Don't you agree?"

Porter: "I don't make the rules."

Lawyer: "Doctor, are you familiar with the term iatrogenic?"

Porter: "I am."

Lawyer: "What is the definition of that term?"

Porter: "The term refers to an event caused by medical treatment."

Lawyer: "In common usage, it indicates a medical error committed by a caregiver—usually a physician. Isn't that true?"

Porter: "As I said, it refers to an event caused by medical treatment. The definition does not specifically indicate an error. Nor does it indicate causation by a physician."

Lawyer: "Is the term properly used if a patient dies from improper administration of a drug?"

Porter: "I'm not an English major. You'll have to look the word up in a dictionary."

Lawyer: "I have…Maureen died because of an iatrogenic error. That's correct, isn't it, Doctor?"

Porter: "I do not wish to speculate."

Lawyer: "The error, this iatrogenic error, was committed by you…Wasn't it, Doctor?"

Porter's attorney objected. The doctor did not answer the question.

The deposition continues. It goes on and on and on.

No further facts were discovered.

No further facts are necessary.

Doctor Edward Porter killed Maureen. He knows it. His fellow physicians know it. I know it.

He should have confessed.

Chapter Twelve

We knew with absolute certainty what had happened to Maureen, and who was responsible. To our genuine surprise, the guilty doctor failed to admit his guilt. He and his attorneys continued to maintain that this experienced operating room physician had been a mere bystander in Operating Room 5. His lack of contrition, and his bullheaded decision to double down on a demonstrably false narrative, genuinely surprised Maureen's parents and me. This surprise, more than anything else, demonstrated our inexperience with American civil law. The lawyer representing us, on the other hand, regarded lying in court as nothing more than standard operating procedure.

The malpractice suit forced the hospital to assess its precarious position. It was, after all, the institution that had credentialed the doctor and everyone else involved in Maureen's death. The decision of its legal team was a foregone conclusion. The corporation remained resolutely in step with the physician's attorney. Maintenance of a united front is the first rule of legal defense.

Want to guess if anyone seriously considered doing the right thing? Like releasing the results of the hospital's internal investigation?

I don't think so, either.

Early in the process, the doctor and the hospital realized two things. One, they might well lose in court. And, two, I was neither an idiot nor a particularly forgiving individual. They took the next logical step and consulted a psychologist—or some other professional mourner—to fashion an effective method of assuaging me. The counselor probably recommended they attempt a soft approach. They'd appeal to my humanity, and what they supposed to be a natural desire to avoid ugly confrontation. That was their cheapest option. Didn't cost anything to try, and—you never know—it might just work.

So, believe it or not, they actually expressed sympathy to Maureen's parents, and to me. They performed this required task with impersonal and meaningless banality.

It was like hearing an apology over a public address speaker.

What a bunch of assholes.

After that, we interacted with lawyers, and only with lawyers. Lawyers are mercenaries, and, like all mercenaries, they wear uniforms and follow orders. Their uniforms are tailored suits, and the orders they follow are standard operating instructions issued from inside fortresses…the fortresses protecting the Business of Medicine and the Business of Law. The mercenaries man the ramparts with the soulless efficiency of robots.

The legal maneuvering lasted for nearly two years. It was a combination of delay, misdirection. manipulation, and dishonesty. Attorneys use mind-numbing repetition as a weapon. They intend to induce feelings of hopelessness.

These tactics work most of the time. That's why they are routinely employed.

The lawyers were teaching Maureen's parents and me a lesson...Instructing us. We'd have to accept that justice has nothing to do with anything except money. The so-called American Justice System is about making deals.

The standard legal education program eventually convinced Maureen's parents.

It never worked on me.

Maureen's parents wanted justice. I wanted justice. Our disagreement concerned faith in the system. Personal revenge was unthinkable for them—in fact, it was abhorrent. They believed the court attempts to do the right thing, and it is the responsibility of all decent citizens to uphold its dictates. They'd accept a monetary award because they believed it was the only punishment they were capable of inflicting. They deluded themselves into believing that exacting financial penalties on an individual or a business would ensure careless actions never recur—as if a court judgement and the exchange of money could protect patients in the future.

Maureen's parents are so naïve.

I believe justice requires retribution. The guilty should not be allowed to walk away after paying a mere fine. They deserve to suffer on a personal basis—suffer as their victims suffered.

I don't believe you can simply buy your way out of personal responsibility.

The legal process sputtered to an end.

Maureen's parents and I received an offer of settlement, the offer accompanied by a letter stating that no one admitted any mistake. This communication declared our case against the hospital and the physician had no merit, but stated the defense lawyers recognized how expensive a court battle would be for both sides. Therefore, they were offering us money to go away. Naturally, they vowed to destroy our case in court if we refused their proposal.

They even pointed out how emotionally difficult continuation of the suit was going to be for Maureen's mother and father.

In other words, a trial would be a public relations disaster for the doctor and the hospital. The negative publicity promised to be more expensive than a settlement.

The lawyers represented Maureen's killer. But now, and for only the shortest period of time, they were prepared to be generous. They actually used the word generous.

Maureen's parents were drained, used up.

Three days before the trial was scheduled to convene, they accepted the blood money. They pleaded with me to acquiesce. I did as they wished.

I thus learned a great truth. Justice must be seized. It is never awarded.

Three million dollars changed hands. Our lawyer took a third. Maureen's parents took a third. So did I.

I donated half a million dollars to charities in Maureen's name.

The other half million dollars will more than support me for the rest of my life. My will stipulates that, after my death, what is left of that money will also go to charities.

I will not live long enough to use much of it.

I am free to do what must be done.

Chapter Thirteen

I am not a violent man. At least, I never was before. Never possessed the aggression necessary for organized sports. Never cared about winning or losing. Had no desire to dominate another individual…or defeat him. Never wanted teammates. For me, a team symbolized compromise and weakness.

I enjoy physical activity, but always preferred individual pursuits—hiking, bicycling, swimming, and skiing. Sought separation from the crowd. Valued solitude above all else.

Maureen changed all that. I enjoyed her company. She felt the same about me. We were grateful we'd found each other. Neither Maureen nor I needed anyone else.

My pre-Maureen life-style prepared me well for what has happened.

If it hadn't met her, I'd have remained a loner. Now she's gone, and I'm a loner again.

Revenge is not a team sport. It's an individual effort. A private, personal activity.

I understand private. I understand personal.

Retribution requires rules. Ethics, if you will. Only the guilty are condemned. Vengeance cannot fall on the innocent. There must be no collateral damage.

The person in question has to be guilty of grievously harming another human being. Further, the targeted individual must fail to accept personal responsibility for his actions. If a person refuses to admit guilt, he obviously never intends to make amends. This is an arrogance that cannot be tolerated.

Therefore, Maureen's killer must die.

The same is true for his mercenary lawyers. That they entered the fray after her death does not exonerate them. They knew the truth, and they attempted to conceal it. Their fate is the same as their employer's.

I cannot allow myself to be arrested, or die, before I exact full revenge. The police are not fools. Investigating law enforcement agencies will rapidly connect dots between the so-called victims. They'll discover evidence leading to Maureen's death in Operating Room 5. And then to me. My quest will end the moment I'm arrested.

Guilty people will escape if I am restrained prematurely. Can't allow that to happen. I am allowed no mistakes.

I have never hunted, nor have I taken part in sport shooting. It would be too obvious if I suddenly broadened my knowledge of firearms. Even more so if I suddenly purchased a gun. That's the wrong option for me.

Truly, I disdain guns. Firearms are the modern, civilized way to kill. The killer need not touch his victim. Physical separation makes killing easier. Almost impersonal. A coward can kill with a gun.

I am no coward.

I will astound them when I attack. Modern man does not expect a physical attack of overwhelming violence. He fears a gunman, someone who maintains distance between himself and the person he intends to murder.

I have to kill—I will kill—with medieval barbarity. I must engage my enemies hand-to-hand. There can be no physical space between us. They will remember me from the hours we spent together—those long hours during which they set a price for Maureen's life. They will know why I have come.

My hands will be on the people who took Maureen from me. I will see fear in their eyes and listen to them grunt and moan as they struggle for their lives. Finally—at the end of their lives—they will learn the price for their injustice.

The surprising part of my plan—even to me—is this: I'm giving my targets the possibility of escape. If they are brave, or resolute, or even lucky, they could well avoid serious personal injury. Physical confrontations are like that.

They don't even have to win their struggle with me. They need only to manage an immediate retreat or fight me to a temporary draw. The delay need last only a few seconds. How much time does it take to dial nine-one-one on a cell phone?

They all have a cell phone. It's always within their reach. These people are civilized individuals, sophisticated in the ways of the world. They are accustomed to receiving almost instantaneous aid.

In spite of myself, I've become a sporting individual. I'm giving my prey a fair chance to get away. Ironic, isn't it? They have a chance to stay alive. That's something they didn't give Maureen.

Chapter Fourteen

I cannot target every person who participated in Maureen's death. My problem is obvious. I'm going to eliminate high-profile legal and medical professionals. When they die, one after another, no one will believe their deaths were coincidental...much less the result of a random crime spree.

It's not like I'm one of those serial murderers who are rarely apprehended because they roam from place-to-place. Those criminals have one overwhelming advantage: they have no personal connection to their victims. My endeavor isn't like that. It's personal. Extremely personal. That's the nature of revenge.

Can't allow myself the pleasure of killing my enemies in the open. Any plan involving public executions is impractical. Such a shame, but I've got to accept facts. Revenge is not a theatrical exercise.

I have to compress the whole exercise into as few hours as possible. I allow myself eight hours from start to finish. I'll take a basic precaution to ensure success...no one will discover the first murders until after the last.

How many murders can I commit in eight hours? When logistics are considered, the correct number is three. That's the best I can do in the time I'm allowed. I have confidence in that decision. It's unalterable.

The plan can be initiated only after I know each of the targets intimately. Each of them has to be where I want them, and they have to be there at the right time. It's going to be a bit of a research challenge, but I'm up to it.

When you limit yourself to three of anything, you have to make careful decisions. Extreme diligence and thoughtfulness are required. I've identified the most disgusting and unconscionable individuals in the whole sordid tale. I'll introduce you to this trio. I'm confident you'll approve of my choices.

After the third murder, the police will begin looking for me, and they'll find me.

Their efforts will gain them but one thing—a front row seat at my suicide.

I accept my fate. I look forward to it. That's my great advantage.

Now, you ask, who will die? Let's go through the list.

We will start with the hospital's corporate lawyer. He isn't a friend of the physician. Much less is he the physician's defender. In fact, he would have destroyed Doctor Porter had that been in the hospital's best interest. This attorney works for the hospital and protects the hospital. Period. He doesn't care about a physician, or for people of any kind. His only concern is a legal entity—the hospital corporation. Justice isn't an afterthought for him. Rather, it's something he's never considered. He believes he has no ethical responsibility for patients because the hospital corporation has none. I will disabuse him of that notion.

The death of the anesthesiologist's lawyer will be even more gratifying. He and I sat across a table and negotiated for hours. We know each other well. Well enough to know we have no common ground. He maintained his client had made no mistake—and then offered me money in exchange for Maureen's life. Incredibly, he used the word generous to describe the position he, his client, and the hospital had adopted. He actually believed I'd betray Maureen for money. That was a colossal misjudgment. Only a man who possesses the amorality of a defense attorney would sell out. I'm not that kind of person. I will teach this legal whore the difference between him and me.

The two aforementioned individuals put a price on Maureen's life. They did this because they believed her life had no value.

Do these men of the law expect me to value their lives?

Finally, we come to Dr. Edward Porter, the man who falsely claims he has no responsibility for Maureen's death. You are familiar with his deposition. We both know what happened in Operating Room 5. It's obvious—and every decent person will agree with me—that Doctor Porter has no right to remain in a world where Maureen is absent.

Chapter Fifteen

It's been six months since I last wrote in this journal. I quit my job and live frugally on the part of Maureen's settlement I retained. It's taken time to become accustomed to not working. Strange not to factor deadlines, colleagues' input, and supervisors' demands into a schedule. I don't file tax returns, pay no health insurance premiums, nor worry about my 401K. I've never before experienced such freedom.

My lifetime will be of limited duration. It's fitting to leave all distractions behind. Only the essential remains.

I spend my time studying targets. I want to know them better than I've ever known anyone else—that is, anyone except Maureen.

There's much to learn.

It's not simple, this in-depth study of people. It's much more than discovering where they work and how they live. It isn't enough to gather intelligence about them—I must understand them. What kind of people are they? How do they see themselves? What motivates them? What scares them? How do they react to stress? When are they likely to be alone? What measures do they take for self-protection?

It'll be necessary to predict precisely what they will be doing and where they will be on a specific day. The day they die.

My transportation, weapons, food, water, and places to wait between strikes must be prepared. When the operation begins, I'll move seamlessly from target to target.

Timing is my advantage. I will wait until everything is right for me—and wrong for them.

They'll continue living their happy, successful, hypocritical, secure lives until moments before they die.

They won't see death coming.

Neither did Maureen.

Chapter Sixteen

Philip Henry Knowles is fifty-five years old. He graduated from law school at the advanced age of thirty-four. The delay in beginning his legal education was necessary because he'd exhausted himself in his relentless pursuit of a bachelor's degree. It's obvious why he'd been so worn out—that B.A. represented six years of supreme effort. The stringent requirements for his degree in communications were so overwhelming that he'd had time for only the occasional party.

Immediately after collecting his B.A., Phil went on vacation. He felt he'd earned a little time off.

The new graduate could afford to rest because he came from a wealthy family. His father had founded a law firm, worked hard, and done well.

Six years after obtaining his bachelor's degree, Phil opened a thirtieth birthday card from Dad. It didn't contain the usual stipend. Shockingly, it contained only a letter. The note, more lawyerly than fatherly, stated flatly that the old man was through financing his wayward son. Therefore, Phil should get off his dead, lazy, drunken ass and support himself.

In an unexpected display of tolerance, Dad promised an associate position in his firm if the little asshole managed to earn a degree from a law school. Any law school. After further negotiation, Dad agreed to revisit his fiscal relationship with Phil—that is, he'd do that after his son successfully completed his first semester of professional training.

Phil had no hope of acceptance at a prestigious university, so he settled for one in the second tier. It's one of those schools that accommodates students who've experienced academic difficulties—and continues to accommodate them as long as tuition is remitted in a timely manner.

Things worked out for Phil. He stumbled through law school and somehow passed the bar examination. Dad hired him, and Phil rapidly discovered his niche. Gregarious, charming, and impeccably dressed, he excels at meet and greet. He looks potential clients in the eye and convinces them he actually cares about their problems. Phil sounds competent as he quotes legal precedents off-the-cuff—all of it bullshit. Everything depends on his clients not understanding the law. That assessment is usually correct.

Phil's a consummate liar. It isn't something he had to train for. He's a natural.

Assistants do the tiresome tasks of researching case precedents, writing legal briefs, preparing negotiating positions, and constructing arguments for use in the courtroom. Artists like Phil don't have time for such mundane grunt work. He's a big-picture person. A mover and shaker.

Early on, Dad's firm recognized his talent, and his shortcomings. Phil isn't a legal scholar and isn't particularly interested in justice—or the law in general. What is he? He's a salesman. Someone who impresses clients. Clients with lots of money and no compunction about using it. Clients whose every move is designed to expand their market share.

Phil's clients are CEOs of corporations.

Philip Henry Knowles is the attorney of record for several corporations, including the hospital whose people killed Maureen.

It's a perfect fit, the hospital corporation and Phil. Neither of them care about right, wrong, or people. They're interested only in the bottom line.

Phil isn't troubled about anything a corporation does, so long as it pays his fees. He concentrates on what is important in life. Money. Specifically, his money.

It takes a lot of money to be Philip Henry Knowles. He'll do whatever it takes to keep it flowing.

He's got two ex-wives, and soon he'll have a third. Then there's that kid starting her third year of college. Next year promises to be even worse. That's when there'll be two additional college-age brats. Those two offspring—whelped almost simultaneously by his wife-at-the-time and a mistress—will be seeking self-discovery. Naturally, his children can only find themselves at expensive liberal arts colleges.

Do you think he regrets fathering two children at the same time? That must have been a bad year—dealing with outgoing wife number one and incoming wife number two. I think it's kind of funny. Don't you?

As he reaches his middle fifties, Phil's starting to wear out. He's trying to camouflage the downward slide of his limited abilities. Bright and ambitious people surround him at all times. Their essential task is to make sure Phil doesn't embarrass the firm. He's allowed to greet friends, to reminisce about old times, and to assure clients that his people are looking into whatever is bothering them. The moment the discussion becomes substantive, young lawyers steer the discussion away from him. He remains at the head of the table and beams magnanimously.

His assistants prepare the groundwork for every negotiation. They brief him on exactly what to say and when to say it. Most importantly, they immediately intervene whenever Phil shows any sign of departing from his assigned lane.

When his law firm defends a hospital corporation in a medical malpractice case, Phil makes the final offer to the plaintiffs. He does this as a respected and distinguished member of his profession. As the final negotiating ploy, he summarizes the true financial value of the deceased person's life. Phil sadly states that it is his duty to introduce the grieving plaintiffs to the real world. In his world—the world of civil law—a person's worth can only be described in monetary terms. That's just the way it is. He tells survivors they must set emotion aside and accept the hospital corporation's proposed payment. It's a good offer. More than fair. In fact, it's generous.

He then—regretfully—makes veiled threats about what his firm will do to anyone who foolishly wishes to press the matter in court.

That's the way he talked to me…The fool.

It's been some time since Phil and I spoke personally. But, since he's important to me, I continually evaluate his situation. It's become evident his downward professional spiral is accelerating. His deteriorating situation makes him more predictable, and thus more vulnerable. Bad for him, good for me.

The firm has long kept Phil on a leash, and the leash is getting tighter. His partners are in a difficult position. They want Phil to recruit clients, but they don't enjoy covering for his ineptitude.

His secretary received orders from the firm's board of directors to report immediately if Phil shows up at the office drunk, severely hungover, or otherwise incapacitated. She makes frequent calls.

His partners' lack of faith, and his loss of status, is embarrassing—even for Phil. He does what he can to avoid confronting his partners. He's even hesitant to question his supposed subordinates. Doesn't spend much time in the office anymore. Comes in only when the board calls him, then does precisely what they tell him to do.

His salary hasn't changed.

He spends weekends, mostly alone, at his vacation house—an expensive showplace on Hawkeye Lake. He's never been much of a traveler, so the fact that the lake is only twenty miles from his townhouse in Des Moines doesn't trouble him. What's important is that he's wealthy enough to possess two houses.

He's lost interest, and the ability, to entertain women. That's probably just as well. They're so damn expensive. But he still enjoys fine wine. He really doesn't mind drinking alone. Much more peaceful that way.

Once upon a time, Phil entertained at Hawkeye Lake to demonstrate his wealth and power. Now he looks out a picture window and tries to convince himself he's still a player.

There'll come a day when I visit Phil at his lovely lakeside home.

He'll learn he's still an important man. At least, he is for me.

Chapter Seventeen

William Ferguson makes his living defending people accused of medical malpractice. That's all he does.

Successful people talk about discovering a meaningful career—one that is both interesting to them and essential for society's well-being. What they describe as a calling. If Bill Ferguson ever made such a statement concerning his choice of legal specialties, he'd be lying. The truth is this: Bill discovered that malpractice defense is an unexploited niche. A highly remunerative niche. He recognized opportunity, went for it, and became rich. His legal skills are average, but his judgment in choosing his life's work was excellent.

Twenty-five years ago he and two other young attorneys walked away from a long-established law firm. That firm's directors didn't appreciate the three's expertise—or their potential.

The disagreement involved money. Every disagreement between lawyers involves money.

Soon after graduating school, the three fledgling legal eagles began working for the aforementioned law firm. Their supervisors constantly assigned them cases relating to medical malpractice. In fact, the corporation's directors tasked them to become the office experts in this specialized field. The three Young Turks sued some physicians, defended others. They'd do anything to turn a buck—that's what attorneys do. It's what they are expected to do. A financially successful attorney is on his way to partnership. Well, maybe he is.

Two years into their employment, inspiration struck. It became obvious to these up-and-coming officers of the court that they'd make more money defending medical caregivers than they could ever hope to make suing them.

It's purely a numbers game.

The plaintiff's attorney in a malpractice suit has to win. Otherwise, he/she doesn't get paid. Sure, plaintiffs' attorneys hit the jackpot occasionally, but such results are rare. The doctor, nurse, or hospital wins most of the time.

In contrast, attorneys for the defense get paid one-hundred percent of the time. They make money whether they win or lose. It's like tapping into a gold mine.

If their client loses, there's usually an appeal. Lawyers get paid for that. If the court orders opponents to reach a negotiated settlement, attorneys are on the clock. Reassuring prima donna medical clients, and counseling them not to take legal matters personally, is another time-consuming task. Time-consuming tasks are lucrative.

Prepping a client for courtroom testimony is a maddening exercise, but tolerable because such preparation requires many expensive hours. It takes a lot of time to produce a realistic courtroom environment. Simulations are effective only if they are elaborate. Experts compose questions likely to be asked by the opposition. Then they interrogate their client in a spirited fashion. The culmination of the exercise comes when experienced courtroom litigators critique the defendant's answers.

Simulation exercises end with a suggestion session. Suggestion sessions often start with a preamble. Something like, "You're going to get your ass handed to you unless your responses are succinct and perfectly understandable to the jurors." Or, "Some of your testimony was contradictory. Much of it was defensive and delivered like a whiny six-year-old child." Fairly often, the legal coach will say, "If you bring that arrogant, superior attitude into the courtroom, plaintiff's attorney will finish you off immediately. Jurors aren't going to like you." Certainly, somewhere along the line, an attorney will say, "Your answer to the third question makes it impossible for us to mount an effective defense. Is that really what happened? If it is, we better settle right now…Think about it. What really happened must be…"

Attorneys make the absurd claim that simulation exercises are not intended to influence their innocent employer's testimony. They insist they are merely offering professional advice on effective interaction with jurors. So much for legal professional ethics. But I digress. The point is that preparation requires exhaustive effort by the defense team. Team effort rapidly multiplies billable hours. Thus it is immensely profitable. That is, it's profitable for the lawyers.

Lawyers gain another important advantage from simulations. They acquire insight into their client's ability to handle stress. This is pivotal knowledge for the defense team. A witness who can perform effectively under pressure is crucial. Much more important than the testimony itself. Facts can be massaged. They aren't as consequential as the smooth presentation of a story that sharply contradicts claims made by the plaintiff. It doesn't matter that the defense theory is unsubstantiated and might just as well have originated in an alternate universe. For lawyers, truth is always subject to modification. What's important is how well the narrative plays to non-medically educated jurors.

The firm's directors—smelling the financial potential inherent in medical malpractice defense—agreed that their new associates might be on to something. But the owners of the practice—the partners—were old, self-satisfied, and imperious. They felt they, and they alone, deserved credit for this revelation. Had they not placed these youngsters on the path that led to an inevitable conclusion? Innovative ideas conceived by non-partners belong to the company. Junior associates are mere extensions of the firm. Really nothing but low-level employees. They didn't deserve a pay raise for simply doing their job. As for awarding them a decent percentage of the growing accounts receivable they were generating—that was out of the question. The partners owned them.

The board chairman stated that inexperienced personnel should be grateful for the career opportunities they'd been granted. Inexperienced, wet-behind-the-ears lawyers are duty bound to enhance the company's profits. Why else had they been hired?

Maybe, just maybe, one of these junior associates—or possibly all three—would eventually be invited to become a partner. At a later date, of course. A much later date. Then they'd get a chance to make real money. Partnership is the overwhelming goal of every young attorney—so thought the board of directors.

Discussions of possible settlement between the practice owners and their disgruntled subordinates dragged on and on. Neither side compromised. Negotiations broke down. Finally, the firm's wise old men invited the youngsters to go ahead and attempt the difficult process of setting up their own office—if they thought they were up to it.

The partners were astonished when their former associates did just that.

The three hotshots borrowed a lot of money and became legal entrepreneurs—a move they never regretted.

Before the doors opened at their new firm, the three decided on the image they'd cultivate to manipulate potential clients, legal opponents, the press, and—most importantly—jurors. They'd be self-confident without being brash. They'd present thoughtful courtroom arguments, but they'd invariably express compassion for plaintiffs, who—quite mistakenly—confused poor results with medical malpractice. These newly minted attorneys would never become visibly angry in court unless they were absolutely certain such theatrics were helpful for winning a case. They were aware that emotion is effective only if used sparingly. If employed at the right moment, a carefully managed outburst would effectively illustrate their disappointment with opposing counsel. Courtroom opponents—that term indicates lawyers, and never refers to misguided and occasionally still-suffering plaintiffs—would be exposed for precisely what they were: unprincipled hacks cynically promoting injustice.

The three stayed in character. Always. With time, the act became reality.

They also promised each other that, if their firm became successful, they'd never abuse young lawyers as they'd been abused. To do otherwise just wouldn't be right.

They eventually lost interest in fulfilling that last goal.

Medical malpractice defense lawyers are not creative thinkers. What they do, over and over, is deny allegations, describe the inherent uncertainties of medical science, stress the complexity of human physiology, and mock the scientific credentials of their opponents. They follow a long-established script, and they win much more often than they lose. Frequent victory breeds complacency and resistance to change. It's not conducive for maintenance of a strong work ethic.

In sharp contrast, their opponents—the plaintiffs' lawyers—must be innovative, imaginative, and persuasive. Patients' attorneys attack authority figures. Therefore, they must utterly overwhelm the defense. Jurors have to be convinced to do something they mostly don't want to do—distrust health care providers. People trust physicians, or at least think they should. Doctors are like airline pilots—you trust them because you have to.

In the legal area, just as in warfare, a good defense is easier to pull off than is an effective offense.

As William Ferguson grew rich, he became lazy, self-indulgent, and more certain of his own intelligence and expertise.

He knows he is virtuous, brilliant, and admired. Everyone tells him so.

His wife of thirty-three years loves him. Or, at least, appreciates his ability to provide. She raised their two kids, got them out of the house, has a personal trainer, and lunches almost every afternoon with one or two of her friends. Possessive, opinionated, and utterly ruthless, she runs a successful marriage. She gets everything she wants, and Bill actually believes he's in charge.

Bill's happy with his life. Wouldn't change a thing.

He doesn't think about right and wrong. Intellectually, of course, he must realize care-givers sometimes fail their patients. That doesn't concern him. Not a bit. His job is to make legal deals so he can live well. Nothing else matters.

He believes there is no morality in law. He's right about that.

But he's wrong about many other things. For instance, he's wrong in his supposition that he's going to die at a ripe old age on the putting green of an exclusive golf course.

He shouldn't have defended the person who murdered Maureen. More to the point, he shouldn't have equated justice with a cash pay-off.

In William Ferguson's world there is no morality.

But, unknown to him, there is a debt to be paid.

Chapter Eighteen

Edward Porter is forty-three years old, the son of a small-town family practice physician. This circumstance accorded him financial security and social standing unknown to his rural classmates and friends. He came to regard privilege and high status as his birthright.

Ed graduated first in his high school class, achieved academic success at the University of Iowa, and attended that same institution's medical school. There he performed credibly, if not brilliantly, and was awarded an M.D.

He decided to become an anesthesiologist.

Why did Ed choose anesthesia? Because real money in medicine is generated by performing procedures, and anesthesiologists spend all their professional time doing just that. You want to determine how financially successful a physician is? Count the number of procedures he or she does.

Now, Ed loves his father and respects him. But let's get real. The old man probably spent half an hour with every one of his patients—getting to know them, listening to every irrelevant thing those folks had to say, and making sure everyone left his clinic satisfied. What did Dad get for doing all that? Maybe fifty bucks a pop. Family practice, and spending too much time talking to patients, is a waste of time.

Determined to secure future financial success, Ed accepted an anesthesia residency on the east coast. It was the first—and only—time in his life he ever lived more than one hundred miles from his hometown. He moved to a surprisingly expensive—though still crummy—apartment in New York City and set out to become a highly paid medical specialist. Nothing would be allowed to stand in his way. He completed a year of internship, then three years of education—a more accurate term would be training—in the art and science of operating room anesthesia.

Ed wasn't satisfied with his newly acquired status as a medical specialist. He decided to up his game. Therefore, he applied for a two-year fellowship in cardio-vascular anesthesia. It'd be a lucrative step up.

Ed's strong impression was that patients undergoing dangerous procedures, such as open heart surgery, expect their anesthesia providers to possess special skills. More importantly, they'd pay extra for those skills. He wanted a high salary, therefore he had to concentrate on high-risk operations. Couldn't afford to waste time on low yield procedures like hysterectomies, hernia repairs, or other humdrum surgeries. He'd not make the same mistake his dad had.

He wanted—needed—to be in the heart room all the time. That's where the serious money is.

How could that be achieved? Succeed in his fellowship. Then he'd be anointed a cardio-vascular anesthesia expert—a highly-paid subspecialist.

There was pain associated with the fellowship—it delayed him from earning private practice money for two long years. The difference between his fellowship salary and the compensation he would have received for performing even low-risk private-practice procedures is measured in six figures. That's six figures each year. For two years.

Ed acknowledged this sobering fact, but reminded himself that—once he became a specialist—his compensation would be substantially higher than that of an average anesthesiologist. He expected to make up the money he'd lost fairly rapidly. He was right. It took just over four years to break even for the two years he'd lost in fellowship. After that, it was all gravy. The long-term financial plan always wins.

Ed reluctantly decided to get married just before he began his final year of fellowship. He hadn't been an unhappy single man. In fact, he loved it. He noticed how attractive he'd become right after he'd been accepted into medical school, and was honest enough to recognize he hadn't suddenly become better looking. Obviously his social success was due to his financial potential. It didn't bother Ed that his partners had an ulterior motive. So did he. It just wasn't the same one.

But marriage is recommended before exploring professional employment. Anesthesia groups want stability. They prefer new partners be married. They can't say that, but it's true. Older physicians are familiar with the temptations of their world and prefer young partners who are constrained by mortgages, kids, and other responsibilities.

Nothing is more disconcerting for the chief of anesthesia than receiving a call at six in the morning and learning an anesthesiologist is unable to work. Medical groups hate surprises, and they hate that surprise more than any other.

Unattached physicians—ones prone to partying—adversely affect reimbursement.

Nothing is allowed to hinder the flow of money. Ever.

So Ed married a nurse. Carrie was—and is—pretty, stylish, and socially-skilled. She said all the right things during Ed's two-day job interview. Everyone she met knew Ed had made an excellent spousal choice.

Ed agrees. He sees Carrie as an asset, personally and professionally. Carrie sees Ed as an asset, too. Unfortunately for Ed, Carrie measures assets in dollars and cents. She's known the couple's net worth from the moment they became engaged. It's something she keeps track of.

Ed got the job he wanted, and the new couple hurried back to the Midwest. Their starter home cost north of four hundred K. Ed bought a Mercedes, Carrie made do with a Land Rover. They became members of an exclusive country club, attended concerts by headline performers, and bought season tickets for University of Iowa football games. Carrie even got herself a seat on the board of a local art museum.

Carrie solidified her bargaining position with Ed by producing two boys during their first four years of marriage.

The two boys have a more difficult existence than the casual observer might expect. They attend tutoring year-round to ensure academic success. Private lessons in athletics and music are constant. The boys are expected to discover a unique talent that will ensure prominence and financial success. Their parents will accept nothing less.

Ed thus acquired all the responsibilities his partners desired.

Ed is serious about his career. Despite his young age, he's already completed a two-year term as the group's chief of cardio-vascular anesthesia. He followed that assignment with a year heading Retention and Recruitment. Now he's on the Reimbursement and Pension Committee. He wants to learn everything there is to know about the business of anesthesia. He's certain the experience will serve him well when he inevitably grows tired of the operating room. He's confident that someday he'll become an influential decision-maker for his specialty. His future compensation will reflect his expertise.

He believes he can influence his fate. I disagree. His fate was decided the day he killed Maureen.

Ed is stressed, and he's exhausted. He won't admit it, but it's true. The doctor has spent his lifetime in a never-ending quest for professional and financial success. The daily pressures of the open-heart room, along with his self-imposed financial obsessions, were adversely affecting him long before that awful day in OR 5. The guy was right on the edge. If other physicians weren't so ego-centric, they would have recognized his damaged and fragile ego.

What is my proof of this? In the operating room before Maureen's death—and during his deposition in his lawyer's office after he killed her—he was impatient, critical, and intolerant. He believed then, and he believes now, that he is smarter than anyone else. He doesn't tolerate challenges, even if the challenge is mild and comes from a trusted colleague—someone like the cardiac perfusionist. He dismisses any plea for him to examine his professional actions. Doctor Ed feels it's stupid and disloyal to question his judgment.

It's obvious he is incapable of introspection. Denial is his fallback position.

Since Maureen's death, he's been floundering. It's true he was never found guilty of malpractice in a courtroom, but that doesn't make any difference. His career is on a steep downward slide. His colleagues investigated him, found him incompetent, and banned him from the heart room. Operating room physicians don't trust him.

It's doubtful he'll ever be allowed to perform another high-risk procedure. That's what happens when you fuck-up professionally. The other docs didn't turn him in, but they'll never allow Ed to make another critical decision. His next mistake might take someone else down with him.

He'll never recover professional status.

He'll continue doing anesthesia, of course, but he'll always be assigned simple cases—the uncomplicated procedures he once disdained. His salary has dropped significantly.

I'm certain Porter's financial reverses are what trouble him. A patient's death, if he thinks about it at all, is unimportant—an event that is regrettable chiefly because it adversely impacted his lifestyle. I'm sure he believes his personal difficulties and Maureen's death are commensurate—thus he is released from further responsibility. That's an incorrect assumption.

All what's written above is background information. You want my conclusions. Here goes.

Porter's not in touch with reality. He'll never admit he killed Maureen. Even in the face of incontrovertible proof of his guilt, he denies responsibility.

For inexplicable reasons, he believes he's an effective liar.

He lacks the introspection necessary to evaluate his situation, but that's not the whole problem. Fatigue from his grasping lifestyle has unmasked a basic character flaw. He's a sociopath.

A sociopath is incapable of learning from his errors. A sociopath never feels guilt.

Such a person does not belong in a position of responsibility.

Carrie Porter, his good wife, has to recognize Ed's faults. I'm certain that she, an individual possessing proven strategic planning abilities, has taken certain steps to ensure her financial security—for instance, retaining personal control of marital property. I'd bet she's taken out a large insurance policy on her husband's life. To do otherwise would demonstrate marital incompetence. Carrie is many things, but she's not incompetent.

She and the kids will be fine. They'll be better off on their own.

Chapter Nineteen

Now you know what I'm going to do, and why I'm going to do it.

This little missive will be continually updated. I'll allow you to accompany me on my final journey.

I predict this literary effort will someday receive a lot of television air time. That is, it will after I'm dead. News producers will recognize my story is compelling, emotionally powerful, and capable of causing a temporary spike in viewership. They'll see it as a reality show, but better than that. Why better? Because all the characters in this story will be dead. They can't make excuses or defend themselves. Nothing can be faked. There'll be no incongruous happy ending.

Just think of it. A reality show that's actually real. The public knows how rarely that happens, and they'll follow updates anxiously. Cable networks will milk this thing for days.

Mass media pundits will condemn people who interacted with me. It won't matter if the accused person and I had only peripheral or superficial contact. With utmost gravity, the empty suits positioned in front of television cameras will pronounce, "The warning signs were everywhere. Why didn't his friends, family, co-workers, or the police department see the warning signs?"

The talking heads on cable news are entirely predictable. They have no personal expertise in anything, but they always have an opinion. They make grave declarations, but never offer sound advice. These so-called experts have 20/20 hindsight and absolutely no relevance in the real world.

It's going to be fascinating. Don't you agree?

I'm certain every word I write will be taken seriously. Studied, actually. Most unusual for a first time author. Who knows? This document may become required reading at police academies all over the country.

I flatter myself, but I'd wager some future writer will recognize an opportunity to make money from my work. He or she will use this—what shall we call it? A diary, perhaps—to write a book. The book cover will include phrases like "Inside the Mind of a Killer."

There'll be nonsense written about my childhood, or my inability to accept the loss of a loved one, or my alienation from society. And there'll be a whole bunch of psychoanalysis by multiple—and supposedly intelligent—students of human behavior.

They'll all reach the same conclusion—I was a disturbed or deranged person. Some of them will even suggest I should be pitied.

It's all crap, of course. I'm the only rational person involved in this tragedy. How do I come to this seemingly outlandish conclusion? I'll explain.

In reality, the people I kill are the irrational ones. Think about it. They inflict injustice, even death, on people, and remain absolutely confident they'll get away with it. The doctor kills his patient and endeavors to lie his way out of the crime. He thinks he can do this despite the fact that every knowledgeable investigator knows precisely what caused Maureen's death. This physician makes up a bullshit story, unjustly blames an innocent cardio-vascular perfusionist, and thinks he's good to go. He does this despite indisputable evidence of his unscrupulous behavior. This goes beyond arrogance. Its delusional. Can anyone doubt his behavior is irrational? Maybe even insane?

Then there are the lawyers. On the day they become "Officers of the Court" they take an oath to uphold justice. But justice is the last thing on their minds. They routinely bury truth. They do this because a client pays them to subvert honesty and morality. I submit this is irrational behavior. Why? Because every thinking American knows the legal system is fatally flawed. It is well understood that lawyers care only about winning their cases. For goodness sake, attorneys actually brag about this. This is unsustainable because a legal system that lacks legitimacy will eventually be overthrown. Lawyers aren't just destroying confidence in the government, they're actually in the process of destroying their own livelihood. I recognize they don't care about the aspirations of their fellow citizens, but I'd think they'd be wise enough to ensure continuance of their privileged positions and personal income. You'd expect them to recognize their vulnerability and adopt a more thoughtful long-term strategy. But they don't. Is their behavior sane?

Now I'll answer two logical questions you'd ask me...if you could. First, is death the penalty my enemies deserve? Is there no other way? You most likely believe I should consider something less radical.

Well, I really have no choice. Think about it. Under no circumstances will society impose sanctions on these people. After all, the doctor is guilty only of incompetence and lying. The lawyers are guilty only of lying. Society accepts incompetence and lying. People expect it from authoritarian figures. The doctor will never lose his medical license. The lawyers will never be disbarred. Imprisonment is out of the question. Sure, the doctor lost money for a malpractice insurance company—which plans for such contingencies and will still turn a huge profit for the year—but that loss doesn't affect the doctor personally. As we've discussed, his salary dropped, and his fellow physicians don't trust him anymore, but he'll always earn enough to remain in the upper five percent. He's set for life.

The lawyers are even more immune to consequences. They'll move on to their next cases without a shred of guilt or the remotest fear of come-backs. It's ironic that witnesses in court will be convicted of perjury if they lie, but attorneys face no such constraints. But, then, lawyers set up the system.

As you see, death is the only penalty I can impose. The system has made sure of that.

The second question you'd ask is this: "Why do you choose a path that leads inevitably to your own suicide?" I admit my choice is unfathomable to most people. I'm going to surprise you. I have not chosen suicide because I fear accountability for my actions. I don't fear punishment. I'm beyond that. I choose suicide because it's the morally correct thing to do. If you are willing to kill, you must be willing to die. That is as it should be. I've made my choice. I'm at peace.

The doctor and the lawyers also had a choice. They could have chosen truth.

Instead, they chose death.

Chapter Twenty

Eleven years ago I was hired as an assistant professor by the history department of Iowa State University in Ames, Iowa. I found a house in the nearby—and still recognizably rural—town of Story City. My money purchased much more house in Story City than it would have in Ames. I hoped money saved on housing would offset the gasoline bill for the twenty-mile commute to campus, and it did.

Story City is a decent place to live. The people are polite, well-educated, and proud of their town. There's not much night-life there, obviously, but that's balanced by a tolerant small town culture that avoids confrontation, pomposity, and other such big-city bullshit. Maureen moved in three years after I did. We referred to the residence as our home, not our house.

I'll live in our home for the next few months—the rest of my life. Story City is just forty-five miles from Des Moines. Nice to have my killing ground so convenient.

I've decided to bequeath our home to a local church. I'll complete and date the paperwork before I execute my plan. Best to divest myself of property before I become a criminal. With any luck, lawyers for the families of my enemies will decide it's unwise to contest my last charitable donation. They'll recognize an effort to seize our relatively inexpensive home isn't worth their time or effort. It's even possible the bereaved relatives of the murdered will think it unseemly to take a small gift away from a church. Rich people almost always fear bad publicity more than they require additional money.

The church knows nothing of my plan, and it won't learn about it until after I'm dead. I never attended church in Story City, and neither did Maureen. Just wasn't our thing. But we witnessed Christians striving to make their community better with individual acts of kindness. Maureen and I were impressed when charity for local unfortunates was given anonymously. This was a shock for us. Not the way things are done in the big cities. We'd both come to Story City with our generation's suspicions of organized religion, but now I'm confident that church members will do the right thing with our home. Some good will come from the gift.

There's only one stipulation the congregation has to fulfill before taking possession of our home. They must spread my ashes next to Maureen's grave. There is to be no headstone or any other marker bearing my name. There will, of course, be no funeral—I can't stand false statements or false emotion. Just scatter my ashes near Maureen.

The emotions of church members can be predicted: astonishment at the unexpected gift, and a burning desire to get the disagreeable final task over-with.

I'm sure there'll be discussion on television and in print media about my desire to be laid to rest near Maureen. Enraged editorialists will insist it's inappropriate to honor the last wishes of a murderous psychopath. The controversy will dominate radio talk shows for about two hours. No longer than that. People have a short attention span, and, really, there's nothing of deep principle involved. Let's be honest. I'll be nothing but ashes by then. The same will be true for the doctor and the two lawyers.

It's remotely possible the cemetery where Maureen is interred may object to my plan. I hope not, but it could happen. I'm confident the practical church members will overcome any such opposition. They'll fulfill their duty. We have a contract. Before they can use our home for good works, they have to honor my wishes. They'll understand, and they'll do what has to be done. Small town Iowans always keep their end of a bargain.

This will all play out after my death. I won't think about it anymore.

I'm prepared for my departure. I doubt the people who mistreated Maureen are as ready for theirs.

Chapter Twenty-One

The internet is an effective instrument, and a frightening one. A determined investigator can uncover every detail of anyone's life. Privacy no longer exists. Everyone knows this, and almost no one cares.

The few people who consider the implications of the web have found a way to rationalize their predicament. They argue that, with so much information out there, any fact or allegation dangerous for their personal safety will be overlooked. It's buried in an overwhelming blizzard of data. Their stuff can hide in plain sight. They're pretty sure that'll work.

This approach comforts them.

It shouldn't.

I study my targets in great detail. I know their history, all of it. Once something is on the internet, it's forever.

My opponents have left a clear electronic trail. I began tracking them with general internet searches. This part of my investigation revealed the kind of information present on routine employment applications. This data is enlightening, and is a necessary starting point, but it's incomplete. An avenger, one intent on discovering true vulnerabilities, must dig deeper. Fortunately, there exists a mother lode of destructive personal detail—social media. Everything I need to learn is there. Know what I like the most? All the damage resulting from social media stupidity is self-inflicted. Remarkable, isn't it, that people enthusiastically reveal so much of themselves to predators like me. My targets provide me with invaluable windows into their lives. It's really quite amusing.

I'm dealing with supposedly sophisticated people, people who should know it's not wise to disclose personal details. Instead, they advertise their habits, current locations, and short-term plans. I'd long realized that teenagers and immature people with zero judgment do things like that. But adults? Adults with something to lose? Assets, for instance? Or their lives? I find their candor incredible.

Family members—who should know better or should have been taught better—are persistent leakers. For instance, Carrie—also known as Missus Doctor Edward Porter—isn't interested in concealing the smallest triviality of her existence. Then there's Mrs. William Ferguson and her two grown children—the wife and offspring of a big-time attorney—who don't know when to be quiet or what to be silent about. It's extraordinary.

Opportunities like this have only become manifest in the twenty-first century. It's a great time to be alive. That is, it's great for a person like me. Only now—for the first time in human history—have guilty people granted an avenger such a well-marked trail.

I suppose I should thank them. Maybe I will.

I'll admit that Phil Knowles seems uninterested in social media. His office maintains such accounts, but he doesn't participate. His discretion actually surprises me. For most people, such good judgment would increase personal safety. Unfortunately for good old Phil, and fortunately for me, he's a drunk. A drunk who spends every weekend at his lakeside home. He's entirely predictable. Murdering him will be almost too easy.

I'll pick him off anytime I want.

Chapter Twenty-Two

I've concluded the ideal time to exact retribution is during the month of January. That time of year the sun won't rise in Des Moines before seven-thirty a.m., and it'll set before five-thirty p.m. Darkness will aid me, and I'll have fourteen hours of it every day.

I'll strike when my targets are most uncomfortable. I can't predict weather, but it's almost certain there'll be severe cold temperatures and heavy snowfall sometime during that month. Deteriorating winter conditions make it impossible for people to scrutinize their vicinity. Sight and hearing are compromised by hoods, high collars, and stocking caps. Agility is degraded by bulky boots and cumbersome clothing. The environment is the primary enemy, and people are determined to avoid weather-induced catastrophes. They worry about sliding into an intersection, or driving into a snowplow, or slipping on ice. But they don't fear personal attack.

My opponents will be compromised by their inability to evaluate people approaching them. Winter clothing obscures body language and facial expressions. Clues useful for human interaction are nearly impossible to discern. This is so well known that no one even attempts to read a passerby's intentions. People distressed by cold temperatures are interested only in remedying their personal discomfort. Nothing else matters. They hurry to their cars, park close to their destinations, and, if the wind is biting, stare down at their feet as they walk. Customary awareness of surroundings becomes secondary. No one expects aggression in winter weather. It's just too miserable to fight.

Heavy clothing will make it easy for me to conceal my identity and my weapons. In an ideal world I'd have a stiff wind to muffle protests and screams, but I'll attack even if I don't have that particular advantage. General Patton once said. "A good plan violently executed now is better than a perfect plan executed next week." I'll keep that in mind.

Today is December 10, and it's beginning to look a lot like Christmas. A modern Christmas, that is, marked by a ruthless determination to sell people things they don't need. It makes me sad that selling is more important than giving.

You've probably concluded I'm morose because this is my last Christmas. That's a partial truth, but it's incomplete. You'd have to factor in Maureen. I miss her, and I'd sacrifice my soul—if I had one—to share one more Christmas with her…But she's gone.

Three other people don't know this will be their last Christmas. Boy, are they going to be surprised.

Chapter Twenty-Three

My tools are ready.

I'll wear a long parka—down-filled, hooded, and dark blue in color. The lower hem falls to my knees. Dark blue doesn't convey the sinister overtones of black, but will disappear just as well in darkness. It's a garment ideally suited for extreme cold. Such a coat is not common in the Midwest, but that's because it's too expensive for frugal Iowans who face only two or three months of cold weather each year. Where winters are more severe and longer lasting, say in Canada, such a parka is common.

The average Iowan will notice my unusual garb. He or she will consider it carefully and come to a logical conclusion: "I don't care how much that thing costs. If this cold snap continues, it's worth the money. I'm going to get one like it next year."

One thought that won't occur to Des Moines residents is this: "I'll bet he's using that bulky coat to conceal weapons." They won't be suspicious of a long coat. Such paranoid thoughts are not consistent with their personal experience. A fellow Iowan never harms anyone. Especially in sub-zero weather. Such behavior just isn't imaginable.

If this were Chicago, they'd feel differently. But it's Des Moines.

I have a black stocking cap and two pairs of black gloves—wool gloves inside of leather ones. The inside gloves will keep my hands warm. The outer pair will enable me to maintain a good grip on the rope while I strangle my adversaries.

The parka has two enormous side pockets. The left one contains a coiled rope fifteen feet in length. The right holds a short rope—four feet long. It's good stuff. Polypropylene and five-eighths inch in diameter. It's supposed to have a working load limit of 294 pounds. I've resisted the temptation to attach handles to the shorter one. Never know, I could be stopped for some minor law infraction and a short rope with handles would inevitably induce police curiosity. Anyway, handles are impossible to tuck discreetly into a pocket, so they're out.

Why the longer piece of rope? It's going to be part of a public display.

I require a weapon for physical intimidation and, inevitably, the infliction of pain. A telescoping baton fits the bill. One like police carry. It disappears when I drop it into the parka's right pocket—next to the short rope. Collapsed, it's less than nine inches long. Extended, it's twenty-one inches. It's made of steel tubing and weighs a pound and a half—a quality weapon, right down to its rubber grip. Ordered it on the internet. Cost less than fifty bucks. It's perfectly legal in Iowa—didn't trigger an investigation because it's advertised as non-lethal. Any weapon that appears to be purely defensive is okay—particularly if said weapon is thought to be useless in the hands of an untrained individual.

I'll also carry a short hatchet, sheathed and attached to my belt. This particular tool is only for unexpected emergencies—like forced entry into a locked room. Never know, someone might barricade himself in a bathroom.

There is a second possible use for a hatchet. It could come in handy if any of the targets mounts a credible defense. That's pretty unlikely. I don't think bullshit artists like these guys have it in them to resist effectively, but I believe in full preparation. Can't chance getting waylaid before I finish the job.

I used Maureen's money for one big purchase—a new pickup truck—big engine, four-wheel drive, towing package, snow tires—all the good stuff. My state-of-the-art snow blower fits easily into the long bed of the truck. It's the kind of rig everyone sees in subdivisions after a heavy snowfall. Not unusual at all. In fact, it's routine.

I thought I'd become excited or, possibly, frightened when I reached the point of no return. I'm surprised I feel neither of those emotions. I'm calm, but there's more. I'm emotionally empty. I've never felt this coldness before, this lack of interest in the world at large. I know I'll do the job. Nothing else matters.

I like where I am. I feel complete. I haven't felt this degree of serenity since Maureen died.

I'm ready.

Chapter Twenty-Four

Mr. and Mrs. William Ferguson received a gift this holiday season. Their eldest daughter, the one who lives in Portland, gave birth to a boy. Finally, they have a grandchild. It's what they've always wanted. The new little boy is more important to them than anything else in the world. That's what they say, anyway. It's all bullshit. I don't buy it. Nothing is as important to these grandparents as the maintenance of their lifestyle and social standing. But, I guess, they can't post a social media statement saying they've just fulfilled the third most important goal in their lives. That'd be tacky, even for Mr. and Mrs. Lawyer.

The blessed event took place December 18. Mrs. Ferguson—Roberta, but please call me Bobbi—flew to the west coast on December 16. It was necessary she be there for the birth. She's commented to her followers about every six hours since her arrival. Had to help her inexperienced daughter, Mariah, through labor, delivery, and probable post-partum depression. Apparently, a thirty-two-year-old first-time mother cannot be expected to possess the usual maternal instincts. Mariah is nearly helpless.

Mom is essential because the new mother's significant other is still weighing the pros and cons of this unplanned experience. Bobbi knows everything will work out. The guy just needs a little more time to wrap his head around his current status. Then he'll move his things over to Mariah's place.

Bobbi—who is very traditional—is hopeful that within six or eight months she'll have a chance to throw a big wedding for Mariah and—I'm sorry, the father's name escapes me.

Bill flew to Portland on Christmas eve and stayed until December 28. He hated to return to Des Moines so soon, but he and his staff are prepping for a trial set to begin January 10. Leaving his new grandson was painful, but his profession is a demanding one. His family knows and accepts his dedication to his clients. It's their way-of-life. It's how the bills get paid.

Bobbi will fulfill her grandmotherly duties, and she'll be just as effective in her new role as Bill is in his old one. She's going to stay in Portland the entire month of January, maybe longer. Mariah and the baby—Bobbi's precious grandson—need her so much. How can she not stay?

Bill Ferguson is going to be all by himself for several weeks.

Hope he enjoyed his time with his grandson. He'll never see him again. Just like I'll never see Maureen again.

Carrie Edwards is socially adept. Gregarious. Friendly. A real people person. She spends hours every day staring at her cell phone. Has to stay in touch because she has so much to say. Just now, she's all bubbly about her trip to Florida. Going to take the two boys to Disney World. The three of them are flying down the first Friday in January. Taking advantage of the final week of school holiday vacation. By utilizing weekends on both ends of their trip, they're getting ten days of fun instead of only seven. Carrie knows how to stretch her travel dollar. She's quite a planner.

She noted on Facebook that the weather service is predicting a winter storm for the Sunday after she and the kids fly south from Des Moines. Thank goodness they have the means to vacation in Florida during the winter. She wishes everyone else could have similar good luck.

I feel equally fortunate. Except I'm looking forward to enjoying the snow as it falls in Des Moines. Central Iowa could well be turned into a winter wonderland. I wouldn't miss it for the world.

The one thing Carrie can't control, unfortunately, is Ed's call schedule. On the first weekend after the New Year holiday, he's taking second call on Saturday and first call on Sunday. Strange that she didn't consider her husband's responsibilities before she paid for the trip. If she and Ed weren't so happy together, you'd wonder if she wanted some time away from him. Ah, that can't be it. They're the perfect couple.

Probably as happy as Maureen and I were.

But the Edwards' family vacation is going to work out. Ed loves his family and never limits their opportunities. He's encouraged them to go on down to Florida ahead of him. He'll join them Monday evening. Carrie opines that Ed would much prefer to take an early Monday morning flight from Des Moines, but it's likely he won't sleep much Sunday night—he is a very important doctor—and he doesn't want to travel in an exhausted state. So he'll sleep-in Monday morning, then hurry to Orlando. He'll arrive rested and able to enjoy precious time with his family.

He's a thoughtful and caring father. Don't you agree?

Phil will get a chance to reacquaint himself with me on a Sunday night. The Sunday right after the Friday Carrie and the boys fly south to Florida. Then I'll visit Bill and Ed.

Looks like we four guys are destined to experience our own interesting end-of-holiday reunions.

Chapter Twenty-Five

It's now seven o'clock in the evening on Sunday, January 5. I'm home. Sunset was at 4:58 p.m. The sky is dark, and the wind's picking up. A winter storm is approaching. I'm entering thoughts and impressions on my computer for the last time. I'll begin dictating on my cell phone after I make this last computer entry.

Soon I'll leave for Des Moines. I'll never return to Story City.

Police will read these words within twenty hours. They'll seize this computer soon after my death. By then they'll have already recovered my cell phone and listened to my final dictations. Authorities are going to be very busy.

As a way of demonstrating my support for local law enforcement, I'll attach a post-it note to the cell phone with that device's, and this computer's, passcode. It's one-two-three-four. I have no secrets. Not anymore. I want everyone to know what happened, and why.

I'll leave the phone in the glove compartment of my new truck. Safe and sound. Cops will rush the phone to a lab and decipher its contents. My dictation will immediately lead law enforcement to physical evidence. Unequivocal evidence. With very little effort on their part, three murders will be solved. And a suicide. No one will be forced to spend expensive man-hours following subtle threads in a complex investigation. It's all cut-and-dried.

When they find my body, will they already know there's been three murders? Or even one? I don't know, but I don't think so. If things go according to my plan, the police will initially believe they've found an isolated suicide. The act of a depressed loner. Another tragedy in an increasingly impersonal urban world.

They'll soon be forced to reevaluate that impression.

I hope the sound quality of the cell phone's recordings are up to advertised standards. I want everyone to know exactly what happened. I want Phil's, and Bill's, and Ed's last words to be audible. The world is going to learn exactly what kind of creatures they are.

I'll place the truck's keys, and my house key, on top of my vehicle's left front tire. It's the first place cops will look—if they look. But let's be realistic. Police officers will surely enter and search the truck immediately after my death. Their method of entry will, most likely, be direct.

I don't care about damage to the truck. The authorities won't be able to sell it anyway. No one wants to purchase a vehicle once owned by a suddenly famous psychopath.

I'll be dead within sixteen hours.

I'll give you one last piece of advice. If you're looking for insight into the meaning of life…quit. There are no great answers. No universal truths. No indisputable moral code.

Rarely, however, there are consequences for acts of injustice.

Chapter Twenty-Six

This is my first dictated message. I'm sitting in my idling pick-up truck and looking at Philip Henry Knowles' imposing house. There's just enough blowing snow to make streetlights hazy. The temperature has dropped into single digits.

It's one of those nights when your boots creak on packed snow as you take the small, careful steps necessary to avoid slipping. The air is heavy, the darkness pervasive. People are hunkering down, depressed and listless. No one is on the streets. It'd be madness to venture outside.

There's been only an inch of precipitation so far today, but the weather service says there'll be an additional six inches of snow before sunup. High winds will create blizzard conditions. It's the wind, not the amount of snowfall, that makes travel difficult. Drifting snow is a bitch.

Hawkeye Lake is a place designed for summer vacations. People come here to swim, and suntan, and water ski. These are not folks who ice fish or figure skate—or personally clear snow. Winter work is necessary, of course. The streets have to be kept passable, fallen trees need to be cleared—things like that. Those tasks are accomplished by contractors. The kind of guy who works a regular job all day, then picks up extra change moving snow at night. A guy who's experiencing some economic pressure and is willing to fight the elements for the upper class.

Most owners of these lakeside houses—better described as elaborate vacation retreats—don't come here during the winter. A few of them might visit during the holiday season, but a predicted blizzard sends them scampering back to their permanent residences. Phil is unusual because he comes to Hawkeye Lake every weekend. He doesn't worry about weather and isn't troubled if he gets snowed in. No one else cares either. His co-workers won't call to see if he's all right. They enjoy his absences.

The street is deserted. No activity, no traffic, not many house lights on. There's not going to be many potential witnesses in this subdivision tonight.

The lawyer's house is lit-up. He's obviously awake. I'm going to walk up his already snow-packed driveway, then turn left on the sidewalk leading to his front door. Phil needs my services. We'll talk snow removal.

I'm ringing the doorbell. Someone's approaching. I can see him through thick etched glass. From this point on, you'll get to hear things firsthand. Bet you'll find the conversation interesting.

"Hello, sir. That's my truck parked on the street. The one with the snow blower."

"What do you want?"

"I'd like to offer my services. I'll come back early tomorrow morning—any time you request—and make sure your driveway is ready for you. Get you to work on time."

"That's already arranged. Sorry…Hey, get your foot out of the doorway. I've already told you I don't need your services. Now leave…right now."

"You don't remember me, do you?"

"Get out of here…"

Grunting sounds. A brief struggle. The door slams.

"Phil, Phil, Phil. You didn't handle this well. But how could you? Your current state is a disgrace. You've been drinking, haven't you?"

"Who are you?"

"You don't remember me? That hurts my feelings. I guess I didn't make much of an impression on you—despite the fact we had several intense discussions. Let me reintroduce myself. I'm the boyfriend you paid off last year. Think, Phil. Think very carefully. The death on the heart room operating room table. The death that shouldn't have happened. Not just malpractice. More a homicide caused by negligence. I'm sure you recall the anesthesiologist. The one who gave the wrong drug. Dr. Edward Porter. Remember now? His victim's name was Maureen…You probably don't remember her name, either. Of course you don't. But you'll remember the payout. Three million dollars…Ring a bell, Phil?"

"That case is settled. You took the money. It's over. Accept it."

"You've been wrong about everything. Now you're wrong again. It's not over."

"What do you want?"

"I want to discuss how much your life is worth."

"You can't…"

"This is a negotiation. We need a facilitator. Anyone here in the house who can help us?"

"Of course not. It's nine-fifteen on a Sunday night." Long pause. "Look, we can work this out. We can meet at my office whenever you want. Tomorrow, even. Any time. Let's reach a fair settlement."

"Very good, Phil. A lawyer to the end."

"I'm trying to be cooperative. If you agree to discuss things reasonably in my office, I'll forget about this illegal intrusion. Let your terroristic behavior slide. Won't report you to police. Like it never happened...So be smart and leave my house. It's really your only choice—the only way you're going to avoid serious jeopardy. You must realize that."

"Phil, don't threaten me. The police will know all about me by tomorrow—I guarantee they will. Consequences don't interest me. I'm beyond all that. I'm living in the here and now. And so are you...Say, that's a really fancy stairway. Wrought iron bannister, if I don't miss my guess. Solid. Strong. Your builder spared no expense...I'd like to get a look at this spectacular entrance hall from above. Let's go up there and take in the view."

A scream. "Help. Help. Help."

A thud is clearly audible.

"You're probably a little groggy now. That's because I just broke your jaw with my baton. Now get on your feet and start up those stairs."

"Nuh..."

"I'm going to keep hitting you until you do what I say."

Slow steps, groaning, and gasping.

"Phil, you're really in poor physical condition. That belly of yours is grotesquely swollen. Do you have ascites? You really should have moderated your alcohol intake. Well, no matter. Let's get to the matter at hand. You, your legal colleague, and the doctor determined Maureen's life was worth three million dollars. What do you think your life is worth?"

Incoherent, insistent babble.

"Wrong. Your life has no worth."

More babble.

"I'm going to hang you, Phil."

Struggle lasting thirty seconds. Several more distinct thuds. Muffled screaming.

"Why can't you accept your death, Phil? After all, you just told me to accept Maureen's. You're such a hypocrite. Now you're going to die with two broken arms to go along with your broken jaw."

An indistinct scream. The sound of extreme physical effort. The faintly audible snap of a rope running out of slack.

I'm dictating again. It's harder than I thought to throw a useless drunk off a second floor balcony. I almost misjudged the rope length. His feet dropped to within a couple feet of the entrance hall floor. Now he's kicking around and making too much noise. People don't hang as fast as I thought. For sure, his neck didn't break. He's slowly strangling. This is uglier than I thought it'd be…I hope he dies soon.

It's been maybe ten minutes since my last dictation. I couldn't stand the struggling. It was very distressing, and much too slow. Didn't know how long he'd take to die. Couldn't wait any longer. I have other places to go tonight. So I ended his suffering. I came here to inflict the death penalty, and I did. He deserved that for covering up Maureen's murder, for denying her justice. However, I will not torture. I know that sounds hypocritical, but that's the way I feel. An eye for an eye. Nothing more

I went to the kitchen and found a set of steak knives. One was nearly a foot long. Standing on the floor and extending my arm fully, I could reach high enough to reach his chest with an upward thrust. The first time I stabbed Phil, the knife didn't go in very far. Maybe I hit the breastbone…Like I said, I'm not a violent man and have no experience with this sort of thing. So I turned the knife ninety degrees and punched it into the left side of his chest. It entered his body easily. Surprised me. Just slipped in. When I pulled the knife out, blood gushed out. A huge amount.

He quit kicking. Now he's swaying back and forth on the rope.

The authorities are going to witness quite a tableau after they break down the front door.

Chapter Twenty-Seven

It's 3 a.m. I'm sitting in my truck at an Interstate 80 rest stop on the west side of Des Moines. I'll take time now to discuss the murder of Philip Henry Knowles.

First, let me say that Phil's death didn't grant me closure—or even the remotest personal satisfaction. It was just something that had to be done. A responsibility. I am intent on my task, and waste no energy on useless emotion. My emotions were exhausted long ago.

Completion of my work is all I have left. My path is unchangeable. I am incapable of sorrow or empathy.

I'm also beyond anger. I didn't express animosity toward Phil. Didn't shake my fist in his face and say, "This is for Maureen." To my surprise, executions don't engender such shallow emotions. We're talking life and death, not some silly sporting event.

Neither did I discuss philosophy with Phil. As I'm sure you'll agree, it would have been impossible for me to convince him my actions were just. A total waste of time. Phil didn't understand justice on the best day of his life. He certainly wouldn't understand it on his last.

Turns out, Phil's murder was a horrible experience…for me as well as for him. Like every other American, I've watched movies and television where the protagonist invariably slays his victims quickly and clinically. In popular-entertainment, killers walk away from their victims with clean consciences and no consequences. That's not what happens. Not in the real world. When I engaged Phil, I wanted him to suffer, and I wanted him to die. Nothing else mattered. But, as I watched him slowly strangle, insight came to me. I saw the truth. His fate was inevitable. Phil brought this on himself. I'm merely an agent. I'm the one who had no choice.

I'll finish my work in the next few hours. My two remaining targets will not escape. There's no way out for them. Or for me. My fate, and theirs, is sealed.

Like Phil, Bill and Ed controlled their own destinies. Their choices, and their greed, made the results inevitable. Their flawed personalities doomed them. If I don't kill them, some future opponent will. It's their fate.

I intend to be more efficient from now on. I'll kill them the same way they killed Maureen—smoothly and coldly. No muss or fuss. No regret. No guilt. I'll treat them precisely as they treated Maureen. Educated people refer to such consideration as professional courtesy. How appropriate.

I'll be dead in a few hours. That's a blessing. I've become dissatisfied with this life. Don't want to linger.

You'll be interested in my activities after I knifed Phil. He died close to ten o'clock. I shut off all lighting on the lower story and went upstairs. Switched on the master bedroom's overhead lights, then did the same in the bathroom. Next, I turned the television on. The bedroom windows are covered by gauzy curtains, and I'm certain the glow of the lights and the flicker of the TV were visible to any curious neighbors. Then I extinguished the stairwell lights.

Ten minutes later, I shut off the television, the bathroom lights, and, lastly, the bedroom overhead fixtures. Obviously, Phil had retired for the evening.

I slipped out the front door five minutes later. Thought about using the back door, but the yard is fenced. Climbing over a fence is more obvious than going out the front door. The temperature had dropped, and the wind was blowing snow horizontally. Visibility was severely reduced. I walked back to my truck, staying in shadows between street lights. Houses adjacent to Phil's were dark, and it's unlikely anyone saw me. The new truck started quietly, and I drove unhurriedly away through the increasing snowfall of an impending blizzard.

Chapter Twenty-Eight

It's 6:30 a.m. I haven't dictated for more than three hours. I'm looking at William Ferguson's house in Ankeny, a suburb on the north side of Des Moines. This is a neighborhood where, despite the fact every family has a six-figure plus income, no one advertises his or her net worth. Solid mid-westerners, private and reticent. Sensible folks who don't advocate conspicuous consumption. Much smarter than Phillip Henry Knowles. People here are careful to stay under the radar.

I'll give you a time line. I know how important that is for you. I left the rest stop an hour and forty minutes ago. Joined a caravan of Iowa Department of Transportation snowplows, along with a few diehard commuters, flowing into Des Moines. I slowly travelled the nineteen miles to my current location. Didn't want to end up in the ditch with about a hundred Midwestern residents who suddenly forgot how to drive on snow. Timed things so I wouldn't reach my destination too soon. Didn't want a concerned citizen or an off-duty cop to investigate a loitering truck in a residential area.

Now I'm sitting in the truck, half a block south of Ferguson's house. The heater is successfully warming the inside of my vehicle, and the defroster is doing a pretty good job keeping the windshield clear. Snowfall is increasing rapidly.

A pickup with a snowplow came to Bill's house at 5:45 a.m. The operator pushed snow off the driveway, then unloaded a snow-blower and cleared his sidewalks. The rig departed at 6:05.

Interior lights began coming on at precisely six o'clock, first upstairs, then down. Bill didn't come out to talk with the snow-removal guy, and the guy didn't knock on the front door.

It's been ten minutes since I last dictated. It's now 6:40. Lights inside the house went out a minute ago. The garage door is going up and interior light shines out and illuminates falling snow. Car lights appear and add a red glow to the background white light emanating from the garage.

I'm pulling into Bill's driveway.

Bill hasn't backed out of his garage yet. Heavy exhaust fumes from his SUV spill outside. He's looking up, into his rear view mirror…His brake lights just went on. Now he's exiting his car. Didn't close the car door. He's standing there and glaring at me. Bill isn't happy, but he's reluctant to step out onto the driveway to confront me. It's cold and windy when you get away from the protection of the garage walls. He's going to stay inside and make me come to him.

I'm going to get out of the truck and wave at him, real friendly. This is what's going to happen: I'm going to walk into the garage and address him from normal conversational distance. I'll let you hear our interaction. Again, you'll have the privilege of witnessing a crime.

"What the fuck are you doing?"

"I wondered if you needed help with snow-removal today."

"Can't you see I've already got a service? I have important things to do at my office. Get out of my way."

"Let me come over closer. It's hard to hear you over this wind."

"I mean it, asshole. We have nothing to say to each other. Get your truck out of my driveway. Immediately."

"Bill, you don't understand. This is a robbery. If you make a scene, I'll shoot you in the head."

"You can't…"

"Reach in your car, pick up the remote, and shut the garage door. And don't even think about jumping back into the front seat. That'd be the last thing you'd ever do."

Mechanical noises as the door closes.

"Very good, Bill. Now kill the engine. Bend over so you can reach your dashboard, use your right hand to push the off button, and do not move your feet."

"How do you know my name?"

"That's a dumb question. Even for a lawyer."

"You're a fool if you think you can get away with this. Do you know who I am?"

"Of course I do."

Silence for ten seconds.

"Um…Look, we can work this out. Take whatever you want. You don't have to hurt me. I'll cooperate. I don't know who you are. I'll never be able to testify against you."

"I'm surprised you don't recognize me. Think carefully. Maybe it'll come to you."

"I meet many people, and the interactions are usually brief. I'll never be able to identify you."

"Bill, I really should tell you who I am. You're entitled. Think of it as professional courtesy."

"Please don't. I don't need to know. I don't want to know. Please…"

"I'm the boyfriend. The guy you paid off after your anesthesiologist client, Dr. Porter, killed Maureen. You recall that case, don't you? The three million dollars you lost—you remember that, don't you?"

"Yes. I remember the case. I'm so sorry about her death."

"What was Maureen's last name?"

"Uh…"

"Ironic, isn't it? You don't recall Maureen's last name, and you didn't recognize me, but you can't forget the money…People always remember what's most important to them. Don't you agree?"

"But…"

"No excuses, Bill. You lost money for your client—a malpractice insurance company. The thing of it is, the money you lost wasn't even yours. But, what the hell. You got paid even though you lost…In fact, you got paid a lot. Let's compare that to what Maureen lost. She lost her life. Is that fair?"

"I'm an attorney. I didn't kill her. Every client deserves a defense. I just did my job."

"Further discussion is pointless."

Physical strikes are suddenly distinguishable on the surprisingly high quality audio recording. There are many of them. Then coughing, grunting, and gasping become apparent. These last sounds are partially obscured by sounds of a struggle. Bodies slam into the car and against garage walls.

The racket of physical altercation diminishes over the next sixty seconds, then ceases. Sounds of movement of air against obstruction ceases thirty seconds later. There follows the quiet noise of intense anaerobic activity—not unlike a weightlifter straining while performing a bench press. This sound is not continuous. It waxes and wanes over ninety more seconds.

Five minutes later, the unmistakable mechanical clatter of a rising garage door is apparent. Its descent follows almost immediately.

Chapter Twenty-Nine

I'm driving away from the house. It's 7:08 a.m.

Things went better this time. Not perfect, not by a long shot, but better. My technique is improving.

My attack was designed to render Bill immediately insensate with a blow to the head. Wanted to knock him out with the expandable baton before I strangled him. You'll conclude I did this for efficiency, and you'd be mostly right. But that's not all I had in mind. I intended to grant him a merciful death—quick and relatively painless. Like the electric chair or a lethal injection. No matter what you think, I'm not a barbarian.

It didn't work out that way. He fended off blows pretty well for a guy in his early sixties. I finally got in one lucky whack that stunned him. Still, he struggled fiercely when he felt the rope tighten around his neck. It's hard to believe how difficult hand-to-hand fighting is. I never understood that before. It was a close thing. Too close. I'm much younger than he was and in better shape. But he fought with desperation, if not with skill. Anyway, he lost, and now he's dead.

I never went into the house. Bill may have set a security alarm before entering the garage. I'd bet he did. You know how those alarms work. The outer garage door usually doesn't trip it, but, if I'd opened the door into the house proper, I'd have heard the pre-alarm warning and a demand to enter the pass code. Within ninety seconds, bells and an automatic phone call would have kicked in. Bill was probably counting on me tripping the alarm right up to the moment he learned I wasn't there to steal his Rolex and wallet. When he realized the game had changed…well, I'm sure he was sorely disappointed.

After pulling the corpse to a darkened corner, I used his garage door opener to exit the murder scene. As I stepped outside, I waved, as if wishing Bill good-bye. Surreptitiously, I punched the down button when I was ten feet away from the garage door. I walked away slowly and carefully, just as anyone does on a snow-packed driveway. Don't know if any observer was suspicious of my sudden departure, but no one approached me. There was no pursuit. I drove away without incident.

I'm bruised, but sustained no broken bones or dislocated joints. I can go on, but I'm fatigued and weakened. It's going to take everything I have to finish this.

I'll do what I have to, no matter what. I really have no choice. I accept my fate. Everyone must embrace his destiny. Don't you agree?

Chapter Thirty

It's now 8:25 a.m. It took me over an hour to travel the twenty-one miles to Doctor Ed's house in West Des Moines. He's obviously home. Someone cleared his driveway, probably no more than an hour ago. Very little new snow has fallen since. There's fresh car tracks leading to his garage. Tire tread marks are still sharp in a shallow layer of fluffy snow.

Time to renew my acquaintance with Ed. Please listen.

Chimes are audible. A door opens thirty seconds later.

"Good morning."

"What do you want?"

"I was passing through, and I thought it'd be nice to look up my old friend. How're you doing, Doc?"

"I don't know you, and I don't have time for games. Whatever you're selling, go away."

"I understand why you're so impatient. You have a plane to catch. To Orlando. Right, Doctor?"

"How did you know?" Pause three seconds long. "Oh my god."

Sounds of a scuffle. The door slams.

"Remember me now?"

"Yes."

"Anything you'd like to ask me?"

"Why are you here?"

"Isn't that obvious?"

"I...I...there's nothing...I tried—I did—I did all I could for your friend."

The sound of half a dozen blows. Deep, ominous sounds. A single yell is audible, then gasping, and, finally, a series of low groans.

"I'm getting better at this, Doc. It's true I still don't kill as smoothly as you do, but I'm improving."

"Please, don't." A request uttered with supreme effort.

"Your lawyer, Bill Ferguson is dead. So is the hospital lawyer, good old Phil Knowles. They both died suddenly."

"No..."

A heavy blow, probably from a kick, forces a sudden exhalation of air. Two more kicks cause similar effects, although the volume of exhaled air become progressively smaller.

"I'm going to kill you too. We both know what you did to Maureen."

"Don't make my boys orphans." Pause. A whimpering voice. "Please. I'm begging you."

Two more kicks, followed by sobbing.

"Ed, you're a coward as well as a liar."

"I did wrong during Maureen's operation. I admit it. Caused her death. I'm sorry. If I could change things, I would."

"Tell me what happened to Maureen. Exactly what happened. I'm recording everything you say. You better tell the truth. The consequences for bullshitting me are extreme...You don't have a fucking lawyer here to protect you."

"I gave the wrong drug. It clotted the bypass machine. When I realized what had happened, it was too late."

"You tried to blame the perfusionist. She did nothing wrong, but, if people had believed you, her life would have been ruined. What about that?"

"I'm a coward. Just like you said."

"What drug did you give Maureen by mistake?"

"Protamine. It should have been Heparin."

"Why did you do that?"

"Carelessness. I was too lazy and stupid to check the syringe after the perfusionist questioned me. I've had to live with that mistake ever since. I regret it more than anything I've ever done in my life."

"That's rich, Doc. In your world a hypocritical apology gets you off the hook. That's not what happens in my world...the real world. I'm not interested in what you've had to live with. Know why? Because Maureen didn't get to live at all."

"I was so afraid. She was dead, and I was sick about that, but I couldn't bring her back. I still have a family to support. If I couldn't practice medicine...what happens to them?"

"Hard to give up a high salary. That's the problem, isn't it?"

"You don't understand the pressures in my life."

"Understand this. I will have justice."

"If you let me live, I'll spend the rest of my life making up for her death."

"You must think I'm an idiot. It's insulting, a bullshit statement like that."

"I'll do it. I promise."

"Your word is worthless."

Another kick. Another groan.

A weak, hoarse voice is barely audible. "Would Maureen want you to kill me?"

Forty-five second pause.

"No, she wouldn't. Maureen was a decent person. Nothing like you. She wouldn't approve of me committing murder. Even murdering you. I'll spare you, but only because that's what she'd want me to do…You're a pitiful piece of shit. Begging for your miserable life. You disgust me." Long pause. "But I will have justice. You're never going to practice anesthesia again."

Two more kicks. Background weeping.

"It's getting hard for you to breathe. Your ribs must hurt awful. I'm going to make a tourniquet out of your belt. I'll do the best I can. Can't promise anything, but maybe it'll stop you from bleeding to death. Do you believe in God? If you do, you'd better start praying. If He's with you, you'll live. If not, you're going to die."

'What are you going to do?"

"I'm going to cut off your right hand."

"No."

"If you say one more word, I'll kick you to death. You're getting a better deal than Maureen did. Accept it."

Indeterminate background noises are audible.

"Here we go, Doc. I'm going to break your jaw because I'm sick of listening to you. I brought a hatchet because I might have needed it if you'd tried to hide yourself in a room. It'll work for the amputation. You'll probably pass out. Well, you will if you're lucky…Going to restrain you with the same rope I use to strangle your lawyer. I'll call nine-one-one when I feel like it. You can spend your time hoping this is the first day of the rest of your life."

Two more kicks. Then a series of hacking noises. Background breathing becomes rapid and shallow.

The door slams.

Chapter Thirty-One

It's ten in the morning. I'm sitting in my truck on the sixth floor—the uppermost floor—of a familiar parking garage. It's across the street from the hospital entrance. I was here on the last day of Maureen's life. Now I'm here on the last day of my life.

They've cleared the streets around the hospital and its adjacent structures. Snow removal at a major health care facility is among the city's first priorities. No matter what Mother Nature throws at Des Moines, the hospitals must be functional.

There's no snow on the street below me. Just frozen road surface. I appreciate what the snowplow crews accomplished overnight. I thank them for their dedication and efficiency. My confidence is complete. There's no chance of survival after I jump. None at all. That's comforting.

The workmen did a great job getting this structure ready for today's business. They pushed snow into piles, making eighty percent of the parking space on the top level useable. I intend to complete my literary work before I leave the truck. That is, I'll complete it unless I see police cars with red lights approaching the ramp. If that happens, I'll cut things short and walk the thirty feet to the barrier wall. I've already checked things and found the perfect place to jump. The wall is only five feet high, and I can easily climb over. I could even stand upright on top of it—its more than a foot wide. That's what I'll do—I'll stand on the wall. That'll add another five feet to my fall. More height isn't required, but I might as well utilize every advantage.

When I looked down from my intended launch point, I saw no structural impediment to my fall. Nothing below but the street. All I have to do is make sure no car's going by. I will not harm some innocent person who's just minding his or her own business. If I hit the roof of a passing car at terminal velocity, injury to a driver or passenger would be inevitable. That's an injustice I will not permit.

Before I leave, I'll tell you about the doctor. I did as I promised. Called nine-one-one and told them where to pick him up. I haven't seen an ambulance yet, but the Emergency Room's around the corner from where I'm now sitting, and I suppose I could have missed its approach. Or maybe EMT's took him to another hospital. Of maybe he bled to death and the coroner is at his house. I don't know or care what happened to him. His fate no longer interests me.

At this moment, authorities are tracing my cell phone. Its number appeared on the screen of the nine-one-one operator. She knew who I was before I said a word. Law enforcement is using technology to find me. They'll be here soon. Police are good at their job.

I'm not going to wait for them. Won't allow my death to become a spectator sport. Wouldn't want the body cam of some officer to record my suicide. It'd be replayed over and over on news telecasts. For fucking ever.

People are going to label me a psychopath—a madman. It's easy to bestow such a label. Doesn't require intellectual honesty or deep thought to place me in a category separate from the rest of mankind.

What the public can't face—refuses to face—is the hard truth. Injustice can drive a sane person to extreme decisions. This is doubly so if that person knows that injustice is so ingrained in the system that it will never be corrected.

I fulfilled my duty. My task is complete. I am at peace.

I believe in justice. I was willing to kill, so I must be willing to die.

I miss Maureen.

My death is my own.

Good-bye.

Chapter Thirty-Two

Three days after the carnage in Des Moines, Police Chief Joseph James conducted a campaign event disguised as a press conference. Though he'd rarely discussed what he intended to do after he retired from law enforcement, his political ambitions had long been apparent. At last, the time had come. No candidate for elective office could hope for a better launch.

The chief wore the no-nonsense uniform of a working police officer—except for the four stars on his collar. A throng of local and national reporters quieted as this serious professional—someone who obviously knew what he was doing—took center stage. Tragedy's first act requires victims. Its second act demands heroes. Fate had smiled on Chief James, and he leaped into his new role.

With utmost gravitas, this wise and unflappable servant of the people nodded to his audience and began the most important briefing of his life. "The Des Moines Police Department wishes to report that our investigations into the murders of two prominent attorneys, Mr. Philip Henry Knowles and Mr. William Ferguson, and the savage mutilation of a local physician, Dr. Edward Porter, have progressed rapidly. These crimes are connected. Our probe is ongoing, but at this time I can state, and let me make this clear, that the public is not endangered by a criminal still at-large. We know who committed these crimes." Pause. "He is dead."

"We have irrefutable evidence that Patrick Stephens, a former Iowa State University instructor, was the perpetrator of these brutal attacks. Police officers, using sophisticated electronic techniques, ascertained his location soon after beginning their manhunt. They found him at the base of the Des Moines General Hospital parking garage—dead by his own hand.

"Doctor Edward Porter is the only survivor of this murderous rampage. His family has authorized us to make the following statement concerning the doctor's medical condition: His right hand was amputated in the assault, he suffered severe facial injuries, and ribs on both sides of his chest were fractured. He required a tracheostomy because his airway was compromised by extensive facial trauma, and his breathing is now being assisted by a ventilator. He suffered catastrophic blood loss due to his severe trauma. Doctor Porter is fortunate to be alive. His family wishes to thank the professionals at Des Moines General Hospital for saving his life. Further updates on his medical condition will come from his physicians or his family, and only from them.

"Patrick Stephens committed the vicious beating and mutilation of Dr. Porter. He murdered Mr. Knowles and Mr. Ferguson with extraordinary brutality. There is no doubt as to his guilt.

"He acted alone, then chose suicide rather than facing consequences for his actions.

"He took the coward's way out.

"Mr. Stephens' personal cell phone has been recovered. Audio data recorded during the attacks is contained on that device. It confirms his role in these crimes. We are also in possession of a detailed diary discovered in Stephens' home in Story City. The diary was drafted on his personal computer. That document, written over a period of several months, details his illogical interpretation of events, as well as the hostility such misunderstanding causes.

"Forensic evidence collected at the crime scenes verifies the audio and written evidence. We know precisely what happened."

Then, ignoring the staged body language of the reporters, their mournful faces, and their repeated gasps, the chief described the botched hanging of Knowles and his eventual demise from a knife wound. James went on to detail Ferguson's strangulation, mentioning that evidence at the scene demonstrated an intense struggle and slow death. Finally, with the masterly touch of a born story teller, the chief recounted the beating of Doctor Porter, the application of a tourniquet—possibly placed to prolong the victim's suffering—and the hacking off of the doctor's right hand with a hatchet.

It was great theater. More importantly, it was great television. The chief wasn't talking to the jaded reporters sitting in folding chairs before him. He'd forgotten them. He was speaking to potential voters watching him from their workplaces and homes. They were fascinated by the intimate details of violence and murder. More than fascinated...they were transfixed. People couldn't take their eyes off Joseph James. A new political star had risen in Iowa.

The chief concluded, "The investigation will continue. We will explore every facet of these crimes. When our report is complete, we will release as much of our findings as is appropriate for the public. Here in Des Moines, we believe in transparency.

"I offer my personal condolences, and the condolences of my department, to the families of the slain and to Dr. Porter and his family.

"I am prepared to answer questions at this time."

"Chief James, have you identified a motive for these crimes?"

"We believe—no, let me make that stronger—we know that Patrick Stephens was distraught by the death of his partner, Ms. Maureen O'Donnell. She died during a high-risk surgical procedure at Des Moines General Hospital. Care-givers intended to correct her life-threatening cardiac condition. The operation failed. Sadly, complications took her life while she was still on the operating room table.

"Ms. O'Donnell, her parents, and Stephens were warned of the gravity and potential dangers such operations entail. Ms. O'Donnell, a registered nurse, was entirely familiar with such procedures. She understood the risks and chose to proceed with surgery. Dire results in such operations are rare, but are known to occur. A small number of patients do not survive.

"Mr. Stephens was unable to accept this fact of medical science.

"He became inconsolable, then angry, when medical staff informed him of Ms. O'Donnell's tragic outcome. He ignored expressions of sympathy and refused offers for grief counseling. Medical professionals who interacted with him immediately after Ms. O'Donnell's death commented on his unusual mental state. He didn't display the usual signs of mourning. A grief counselor commented on his cold anger. His rage was palpable. Mr. Stephens frightened her, and she separated herself from him as soon as she could. Stephens voiced no direct threats to hospital staff, nor did he display overt signs of instability. Therefore, no immediate medical intervention into his mental state could be initiated. He did not meet the legal criteria necessary to mandate involuntary psychiatric care. No one could prove he was an immediate threat to himself or others.

"The grief counselor believed, and fervently hoped, she'd witnessed a temporary reaction due to Ms. O'Donnell's sudden and unexpected passing. She believed she'd witnessed a temporary stage in this man's grieving process, an intermediate phase that would inevitably lead to acceptance of his partner's death. Sadly, she was incorrect in this assumption.

"Stephens came to believe the operating-room staff, and, in particular, Dr. Porter, were responsible for Ms. O'Donnell's death. He was one of the plaintiffs in a malpractice suit filed against the doctor and the hospital. Other plaintiffs were Ms. O'Donnell's mother and father. The case settled out-of-court. The plaintiffs received a substantial sum of money from the malpractice insurance company. Everyone involved accepted the court's decision and made peace with the tragedy. Everyone, that is, except Stephens.

"William Ferguson defended Dr. Porter throughout the legal process. Philip Henry Knowles represented the hospital. These circumstances establish Mr. Stephens' relationship with the other victims of his crime spree.

"The police department consulted a psychiatrist in an attempt to understand Stephens' evolution from dedicated educator to violent predator. The psychiatrist—I'm not at liberty to reveal her name because she never met Patrick Stephens—cautioned us that her opinion is purely conjectural. She is involved only because the police department requested her aid. She helped us because she felt a duty to do so. She did not accept remuneration. We thank her for her efforts.

"The doctor thinks it possible that Stephens' mental imbalance resulted from his encouragement of—or, at least, his agreement to—Ms. O'Donnell's decision to proceed with surgery. If this is so, he likely felt guilt concerning her death. This is one plausible explanation for the unfathomable. But it is, by no means, definitive. We will never know precisely what went wrong with Patrick Stephens. All we know is that this previously unremarkable man became a cold-blooded killer."

"Chief, you've spoken about personal interactions and probable motive. How did you reach such in-depth insight into the mind of Patrick Stephens so quickly?"

"His personal statements—the diary and voice recordings to which I previously alluded—are detailed. In fact, he unwittingly documents his accelerating mental deterioration. Stephens, like many terrorists and madmen, felt a compulsion to explain himself. Perhaps he wanted forgiveness, or at least sympathy. His complaints about powerful actors, like physicians, hospitals, and the court system, are rambling and incoherent. He somehow believed he, and he alone, understood ethics and morality.

"Stephens didn't understand the competing and interacting factors that determine outcomes in our justice system. Nuances and complexities baffled him."

"He was a disturbed individual."

"Is the claim that Dr. Porter committed malpractice genuine?"

"The malpractice allegation was not proven in court. Settlement was reached before a trial could take place. No one can accurately comment on the suit's validity. Court documents for that civil lawsuit are sealed. Dr. Porter and his attorneys denied the charge. There will be no more investigation into the circumstances of Ms. O'Donnell's death. Her parents, grief-stricken but sane, abided by the terms of the settlement, so we can infer they felt it was fair. Mr. Stephens did not agree with them, even though he accepted a considerable amount of money from the malpractice insurance company."

"Chief James, when will authorities release Patrick Stephens' communications?"

"Only after the investigation is complete. Anything released will be heavily redacted. We do not believe releasing unedited versions of his diary or his audio recordings is in the public interest. Doing so might prove detrimental to members of our society who are of marginal stability. Remember, the man who created this record was delusional, disturbed, and murderous. Stephens believed his words were significant. He boasted that his message would generate wide public interest. We disagree, and we intend to deny him posthumous celebrity. We do this out of respect for his victims."

"Has Doctor Porter been able to aid the investigation?"

"No. Doctor Porter's life-threatening injuries necessitated immediate surgery when he reached the hospital. He is now receiving care in the Intensive Care Unit, and has been unable to communicate. We will interview him when his physicians deem the time is right."

"Was Doctor Porter alone at the time of the attack?"

"Yes."

"If he was alone and unable to communicate, who notified emergency services of his medical status?"

"A nine-one-one operator received a call detailing his condition and location."

"Who made the call?"

"The call came from Patrick Stephens' cell phone."

The questioner's face registered surprise. Then, seemingly oblivious to the sudden increase in background noise, he went on, "You neglected to tell us that in your opening statement, Chief…Is requesting aid for his victim unusual behavior for a murderer?"

"Yes."

"When were you going to tell us about that?"

"It will be in the completed report."

"Huh…Chief, what conclusions do you draw from Stephens saving the life of the doctor?"

"Stephens injured the doctor in the first place, so he doesn't deserve credit for saving him…Look, I'm not a psychiatrist. I can't look into a criminal's mind."

"I'm looking forward to seeing the complete report, Chief."

"I'm looking forward to giving you as much information as I can."

The press conference went on for another hour. Reporters became bored as the conference devolved into the usual format. Numerous self-described journalists made repetitive observations so they could appear on camera. No original questions were posed, and no further insight into the crimes was offered. Chief James eventually looked into the television cameras, promised he'd be in touch, and walked importantly off the dais.

Chapter Thirty-Three

Joseph James had, with grace and good sense, ended the press conference before anything bad could happen. Sooner or later, if he'd stayed at the podium, someone would ask something he didn't want to answer. Then he'd have to ad lib—a classic recipe for political disaster. The chief knew emerging political candidates were rarely criticized for saying too little. What got them in trouble was talking too much. He wouldn't make that mistake.

He took the elevator to the top floor of police headquarters and walked to his corner office. High-ranking officers congratulated him on his performance. Said he represented them admirably. He knew that was true, and he was certain his future was unlimited.

All he had to do was not screw up.

His secretary stood as he approached her desk. She said, "I received a phone call for you five minutes ago. The caller requests you return his call immediately."

The chief, exhausted from his first campaign rally, growled, "Call whoever it is and get rid of him. I have a lot to think about."

"Chief, the call was from Daniel Bailey."

Daniel Bailey, editor-in-chief of a Des Moines newspaper, is not a man to be put off. Particularly by someone who will soon be running for elective office.

Chief James dialed the number and said, sincerely, "Dan, what can I do for you?"

"First let me say, you did a wonderful job today. You look good in front of a camera."

"Thanks, Dan. Just doing my job."

"You did it well...But there's this one thing. It's about releasing Stephens' diary and recordings. You said you'd release only what you deemed fit for public consumption."

"We have to do that, Dan. That's how we do business." Chief James did his best to sound self-confident, but his weariness had been replaced by slight nausea.

"Joe, that's going to be a problem for you."

The chief's throat tightened, "Why?"

"Because this morning we received a flash drive and a cell phone in the mail. From Patrick Stephens. Looks legit to us. He even enclosed some hair so we could do a DNA test to ensure its authenticity. It's a complete computer file. Probably the same file you guys seized at his home. Even more interesting, it looks like he carried a second cell phone with him while he was criminally engaged. The audio quality is good. Outstanding, actually. It would seem he went by a postal box on his way to the hospital parking garage and dropped it in. My technical people are all over it. It looks genuine."

"You can't release that information."

"Yes, we can. Our legal team is reviewing precedents, and I'm certain we're on solid ground."

"We'll go to court to block it. Our investigation is not complete."

"Come on, Chief. The investigation is complete. You're just going through the motions. We both know that...Go to court. Ask for an injunction. That'll raise our readership. We'd appreciate you're doing that as soon as possible. How about tomorrow?"

"You can't..."

"We can, Chief. I'm just giving you a head's up. A courtesy call. We always do what we can to support our local police." Pause. "Joe, you're new in the public eye. Let me give you a little advice. It's always wise for ambitious people to get in front of things like this."

Click.

"Well, fuck," muttered the Chief of Police.

Chapter Thirty-Four

Half an hour before sunset, Ben and Sarah O'Donnell visited their daughter's grave. Maureen had been gone more than four years. They stood together, talked about the past, and considered what might have been. The couple didn't cry, or fall to their knees, or question God. Iowa farm people accept the world as it is.

They were alone. It was necessary they be alone.

Just before dusk faded to darkness, Ben reached into a satchel, the one the church deacon had given him, and removed an urn. His hands trembled and he felt tears go down his cheek. He looked into Sarah's wet eyes.

Together they spread the ashes over Maureen's grave.

They didn't do this for Patrick. Ben and Sarah hadn't approved of what he'd done and never talked about him. They'd tried to erase him from their memories, but that didn't work.

This was for Maureen.

In his way, Patrick had loved Maureen. She loved him. She'd want him with her.

Mother and father walked back to the truck, hand-in-hand.

Ben and Sarah never spoke about this. No one else need know what had happened in the small Iowa cemetery, after sunset, on a warm June night.

The moment belonged to them.

Acknowledgements

Patricia, my wife, I appreciate your support and encouragement. You remain my dialogue coach, and your advice is thoughtful and insightful. For me, the most enjoyable part of writing has always been our daily discussions concerning the novel's progress. You keep me on track and ensure my characters stay in the real world. I value your input, and I enjoy your company. Thank you.

Aaron Beaty, I appreciate your expertise, professionalism, and sense of humor. Your understanding of cardio-vascular bypass, and your ability to convey that understanding to me, were essential for this work. Thank you, my friend.

Made in the USA
Lexington, KY
26 November 2019